DYING FOR GOLD

A GOLD DIGGER MYSTERY ~ BOOK ONE

DIANA ORGAIN

D1519925

Lemonade
Press

OTHER TITLES BY DIANA ORGAIN

Third Time's a Crime If only love were as simple as murder...

ROUNDUP CREW MYSTERY SERIES

Yappy Hour Things take a *ruff* turn at the Wine & Bark when Maggie Patterson takes charge

Trigger Yappy Salmonella poisoning strikes at the Wine & Bark.

IWITCH MYSTERY SERIES

A Witch Called Wanda Can a witch solve a murder mystery?

I Wanda put a spell on you When Wanda is kidnapped, Maeve might need a little magic.

Brewing up Murder A witch, a murder, a dog...no, wait...a man..no...two men, three witches and a cat?

COOKING UP MURDER MYSTERY SERIES

Murder as Sticky as Jam Mona and Vicki are ready for the grand opening of Jammin' Honey until...their store goes up in smoke...

Murder as Sweet as Honey Will the sweet taste of honey turn bitter with a killer town?

Murder as Savory as Biscuits Can some savory biscuits uncover the truth behind a murder?

CHAPTER ONE

"I think your store is haunted," Mrs. Jeffries, one of our best customers, screeched.

"It's not haunted," I said.

"Well, the nugget I was just looking at disappeared out from under my nose! How do you explain that?" she demanded.

"Wendy," I offered as way of explanation, pulling the diamond-encrusted gold nugget out of my sister-in-law's hands and passing it to Mrs. Jeffries.

Wendy simply batted her false eyelashes and gave a wicked grin. "I couldn't resist. Isn't it the most amazing thing you've ever seen?"

The store in question was *The Nugget*. Daddy's family had been part of the original gold rush of 1849. Our family went way back, especially by California standards. I was the fifth generation of a mining family, and *The Nugget* had kept our family in gold even when our mine, *The Bear Strike*, had been forced to close in 1942 to support the war effort.

I don't know that I've ever seen Daddy happier than when the price of gold shot up a few years back and it would finally be profitable to reopen the mine.

Ordinarily, *The Nugget* catered to tourists, but I'd convinced Daddy to use the shop as a backdrop to put my best friend, Ginger's, exquisite jewelry designs on display, and all our best customers and neighbors had come out for the occasion.

Dad came around from behind the counter. "Cut the champagne off," he said under his breath.

I laughed. "Daddy! This is a ladies' gathering. One of the main draws beside Ginger's designs is the champagne."

He leaned into me. "Key word being *ladies*. Do you see how they're acting?"

I couldn't deny that there was a lot of shrieking going on and that the general timbre in the room was reaching an ear-shattering pitch. "You're just mad that they're so excited about Ginger's design and not your gold," I teased.

Dad's idea of jewelry was literally a nugget hanging off a chain, and the chain, of course, must be gold. There was nothing more appealing to him. The rougher the nugget, the more gorgeous Dad thought it was. I had to admit that our regular clientele of tourists seemed to agree.

They loved buying a "gen-u-ine" gold nugget that had been mined from California's oldest and still active mines.

Ginger came out of the back room cradling a sapphire necklace she'd taken to fix that'd been broken a moment earlier when two customers yanked it out of each other's hands. The pendant of the necklace was designed as a huge calla lily with delicate gold leaves and a brilliant-cut sapphire as the blossom. The necklace was almost as beautiful as Ginger herself.

She had honey-ginger colored hair and wore a form-fitting dress that hugged every generous curve. The dress was indigo, and knowing Ginger, it was no coincidence that it perfectly matched both her eyes and the expensive sapphire she now held in her hand.

She stood between the customers, Mrs. DeLeon and Mrs. Harvey, nervously glancing at me. "Uh, Frannie? Can you—"

"It's for me," Mrs. DeLeon said, grabbing at her pocketbook.

"No. You. Don't!" Mrs. Harvey howled. "That piece is for me. Wendy and I have been talking about it for ages!"

All heads turned toward my sister-in-law, Wendy, who dutifully wrinkled her button nose, then admitted, "I did tell her I thought there was a special piece she would like." Wendy avoided Mrs. Harvey's wrath by taking great interest in the passing waiter. "Oooh! Is that pâté?"

We'd hired an upscale catering service, *Bites & Bread*, for the event, and judging by the trays being offered to our customers, I could already hear Dad complain about the bill that was sure to be anything but *bite*-size.

However, he hadn't really had a choice. The competitor caterer was *Golden Grub*, run by mother and after their horrible divorce, Dad would rather stick himself in the eye with hot pokers than give my mother any business. Plus, he'd said over and over that Mom was just waiting for her moment to poison him...given their animosity I couldn't blame him.

The waiter, who was about all of eighteen, held the tray out for Wendy as Mrs. Harvey took a great inhale, then puffed out her cheeks. She let the air out slowly, breathing all over the canapé tray.

"I'm going to have to speak to Mr. Peterson! George!" she wailed.

Dad appeared with a smile on his face. He was ever the charmer, but I could tell by the fine lines around his eyes that he was tired. One more complaint from the wealthy, pampered socialites this party had attracted and he might blow a gasket.

"Mrs. Harvey. Whatever is the matter? More champagne?" he offered.

I bit back my laugh.

So much for cutting off the champagne!

"George. Will you please inform Mrs. DeLeon that the sapphire necklace is for me?"

Dad grabbed the arm of another waiter, this one a redhead who worked regularly at the *Bites & Bread Bakery*, and pulled a bottle of champagne out of her hand. He topped off Mrs. Harvey's glass. "Sapphire?" He frowned. "Mrs. Harvey. You and I must have a talk." He glanced around, all the ladies suddenly craning their necks to get an earful. "In private," he mumbled, leading her toward the glass case that held our most expensive gold jewelry.

Dad handed me the champagne bottle, then took Mrs. Harvey's elbow, leading her to the back of the store as he chatted with her, tilting his head close to hers so his mouth was near her ear. She suddenly erupted into a fit of giggles, then whacked my father on his shoulder. I noticed her hand lingered on his arm, giving him the occasional squeeze.

Didn't she realize she was the one being squeezed?

Mrs. DeLeon said, "Quick, Frannie. Ring me up for the sapphire necklace so I can get out of here and away from Mrs. Harvey."

I topped off Mrs. DeLeon's flute. "I think she'll change her mind altogether about the necklace. Don't worry."

Mrs. DeLeon handed me her platinum American Express. "I'm not taking any chances."

I took the card and nodded. "It is a beautiful piece. I'm sure you'll be very happy with it."

Ginger beamed as I rang up the necklace. "I can't believe this is happening. Everyone loves my stuff."

"I knew they would. It's beautiful," I said.

Wendy slipped up next to us. "Totally unique," she agreed. "I'm so glad I convinced George to have the party. What a great idea I had!"

Ginger and I exchanged a look. Actually, the idea of hosting an exclusive sale of Ginger's handcrafted designer jewelry had been mine, but we both knew Wendy would take credit wherever she could get it.

I rang up Mrs. DeLeon and placed the beautiful sapphire necklace into a black velvet gift box.

Wendy and Ginger circulated around the crowd, and Dad popped open another champagne bottle while chatting with Mrs. Harvey.

As I finished helping Mrs. DeLeon, she leaned in and grabbed my hand. "When are we going to see a ring on this finger, Frannie?"

I flushed. For some reason, I hated being the center of attention. I'd much rather people notice the sparkling gold nuggets beneath the glass counter than my hand above it.

"It's getting to be about that time, isn't it, dear?" Mrs. DeLeon asked.

I slipped my hand out of her grasp and feigned a smile. Even though I was hoping for a proposal soon, I wasn't about to share the details of my private life. "When he's ready, I'll be ready," I said.

Mrs. DeLeon gave a throaty chuckle. "Well, my dear, don't wait too long. I know your father is dying for some grandbabies to help out with *The Bear Strike*. Speaking of grandbabies, where did Wendy fly off to?" Mrs. DeLeon turned to look for Wendy.

Oh, good. She could go bug Wendy about getting pregnant soon and that would get me off the hook for the moment.

"Over there," I said, pointing toward Wendy's slender form. "No baby bump yet . . ."

Wendy turned toward me as if she'd sensed we were talking about her. I winked and wiggled my eyebrows, indicating that Mrs. DeLeon was about to descend on her.

She gave me her best "you'll pay for this" look, then smiled as Mrs. DeLeon approached.

I took the opportunity to slip to the back and dial my boyfriend, Jason. We'd been dating for almost a year, and he'd recently been hinting around the idea of marriage, asking my ring size and whether I preferred white gold or yellow.

Which actually was a silly question for a gold heiress. While gold could be many colors, including black or purple, nothing compared to those flakes colored like the sun. But hey, if being agreeable to pink or red gold would get a ring on my finger, I was all for it.

In fact, Jason had been mysterious about this evening. He'd mentioned a romantic dinner and a *surprise*.

I dialed his number and waited for him to answer. It rang four times, and then his voicemail kicked on.

Where was he?

It wasn't like him not to pick up.

Maybe he's shopping.

I imagined him haggling with a jeweler across the glass counter. No, that wasn't likely. Surely if Jason was getting ready to propose, he'd have asked Ginger to design the ring. And yet, she hadn't mentioned a thing.

Footsteps approached, and I tried to hide the smile that was bursting through.

Wendy appeared before me. "What are you grinning at? Siccing Mrs. DeLeon on me?"

I laughed. "Oh, Wendy. Sorry. I couldn't resist, plus she was pestering me about when Jason is going to pop the question."

"It better be soon. He'd be an idiot to let you go." Wendy suddenly took a step back and evaluated me. "What style dress do you want?"

I inwardly cringed. Wendy's new hobby was sewing, and she fancied herself a dress designer, but the truth was she barely knew the difference between a straight stitch and a whip stitch.

She grabbed the fabric measuring tape that was constantly slung around her neck these days and moved toward my waist.

I stepped back. "Wait, wait. Let's not jinx anything. It just that he's been hinting around and he's making me dinner and tonight—"

Wendy squealed and wrapped her arms around my neck. "OMG! You'd better call me first thing."

The sound of high heels clicked on the tile floor. "Call you first about what?" Ginger asked.

"She'll call me first after the proposal," Wendy said.

Ginger and Wendy were on-and-off-again friends and sometimes got a little competitive when it came to attention from me. I suddenly found myself in a tug of war between the two.

"She'll call me first!" Ginger said. She quirked an eyebrow at me and said, "Right? I'm her best friend."

Wendy stepped in and put an arm around my shoulder. "Well, I'm her sister-in-law. Family trumps friends; everyone knows that."

Ginger grabbed my other arm. "No. Not true— "

I wrapped an arm around each of their shoulders. "Okay, as soon as he asks, I'll conference you both or"—I laughed—"send you a group text."

Dad popped his head into the back room. "For goodness sake! What are the lot of you doing back here? I have biddies bidding on baubles, ready to overpay and rip each other's gizzards out over these trinkets. Now get out there and close those sales!"

We laughed.

"Great pep talk, Dad," I said.

He ignored our laughter and began to usher us toward the sales floor. "Hurry now, Mrs. Harvey needs to be rung up for the nugget I just sold her."

Ginger looked offended. "But I thought she was interested in the emerald tennis bracelet I designed for her." She scurried off behind Dad.

Wendy and I followed, but she hung back a bit and said to me, "I got a text from Ben." She rolled her eyes. "You'll never believe it, but more changes for Living History Day."

Living History Day was an annual event where the entire town dressed up in 1850s garb that Wendy helped sew. It was a huge fair complete with sawmill demonstrations, tours of famous gold mines, historic reenactments, and gold panning. And, of course, lots of tourist memorabilia and junk food, topped off with a healthy dose of live music.

Our mutual friend, Ben, and his band *Oro Ignited* played every year.

"What's going on?" I asked.

Mrs. Jeffries, still clutching the diamond-encrusted gold nugget, spotted me and waved frantically at the glass counter. "Frannie! Show me those gold coin earrings! I think they'd make quite a match with this knickknack." She wiggled her wrist so the nugget moved back and forth hypnotist-style.

I moved across the sales floor and behind the counter as Wendy followed me.

"His band's been canceled," Wendy said.

I pulled the earrings for Mrs. Jeffries, who was now absorbed in our conversation.

Mrs. Jeffries pursed her lips. "More problems with Living History Day?"

"Problems with Dale Myers more specifically," Wendy answered.

Dale Myers was the new chairman for Living History Day.

"Dale Myers!" Mrs. Jeffries spat. "That man is making so many enemies. Why, I wouldn't be surprised if he winds up murdered! Did you know that my dear Mr. Jeffries and I were all set to sing for the event?"

"Were?" I repeated.

Mrs. Jeffries nodded, her expression changing to resemble that of a moping child. "Dale said that there were already too many acts scheduled and that he'd have to bump Edmond and me off the list.

Can you imagine? We've been singing on Living History Day for twenty-five years." She crossed her arms with a huff. "Not a very nice thing to do to us when we've just reached our quarter-of-a-century singing anniversary."

Wendy shook her head. "It's downright cruel if you ask me. Such a shame."

The Jeffries were by no means an act that would make it on Broadway. But they had a familiar, hometown sound and I couldn't imagine Living History Day without it.

"That's strange he would say that there are too many performers," I remarked. "I mean, if you two got bumped off the program and now Ben's band too, we won't have any entertainment."

Mrs. Jeffries looked down at the earrings Wendy had just handed her. "You're exactly right." She released a long-suffering sigh as she held the earrings up so that they sparkled in the sunlight streaming through the window. "I came in here to forget about all this. But Dale Meyers's doom and gloom managed to follow me here too."

Wendy offered a sympathetic smile. "I'm sorry about that. But don't you love those earrings? They're just the thing to cheer you up."

Mrs. Jeffries' face brightened considerably. "Yes.. . . . yes, I think you're right. I'll take them, Wendy!"

I barely hid my laughter at how quickly Mrs. Jeffries was consoled by the purchase. I supposed that it didn't matter what sold Ginger's jewelry so long as the afternoon was a success. Still, Dale Meyers had cast quite a shadow, and it seemed Ben wasn't the only one who was unhappy about it.

CHAPTER TWO

*a*t six p.m., we finally ushered everyone out of the store. Three cases of champagne later, we'd rung in one of our best nights for fine jewelry. Dad was grudgingly pleased, even if gold had taken a back seat to fine stones for one day.

Ginger was beside herself, squealing every three minutes. "We need to go out and celebrate!"

"I have a date with Jason," I said, pressing my hand against my tummy to quell the butterflies.

Tonight could be the big night!

"Right, right," Ginger said. She glanced over at Wendy. The two never went out without me, but it seemed that the day had been so successful that they might be gearing up for it. "Well, do you want to get a glass of Chardonnay with me over at the Wine Jug?"

Wendy shrugged. "Sure, why not? I've tolerated you all day. I might as well tolerate you a little longer." Ginger giggled as if Wendy had been joking.

I pinched Wendy. "Be nice."

Wendy laughed. "Okay, I'm just kidding. Besides we need to be together so you can call us when you get your big news."

I slipped my cell phone into my pocket.

"Don't worry, I'll call you guys. How late will you be at the Wine Jug?"

"Late," Ginger said. "We're celebrating. We're going to be late."

Wendy glanced at her watch. "Well, my darling husband will be home from the mine—"

Ginger grabbed Wendy's arm. "No you don't. If we go to the Wine Jug together, you can't ditch me."

"I'll walk with you guys since it's on my way to Jason's," I said, wiggling my fingers in Dad's direction.

Dad, who was closing down the final till, said, "See you in the morning. Don't stay out too late."

I hadn't exactly told him that I expected Jason to propose tonight. I knew Dad wasn't very fond of the idea of Jason and me getting married. Dad wanted me to marry again, sure, but Jason's career goals were not part of Dad's overall plan. Dad had made it clear that he wanted me to stay in Golden and run *The Nugget*, and Jason was in line for a promotion and the new position included moving to New York City.

As it happened, I personally loved the idea of moving to New York. The Big Apple was glamorous: skyscrapers, fine dining, Fifth Avenue department stores with designer names, theater, and opera.

All we had designer in Golden were secondhand goods sold in a small store around the corner from *The Nugget*. If you wanted to do any real shopping, you had to head down the Sierra foothills and into Sacramento to hit a mall. But even then, it wasn't nearly as sophisticated as New York.

Ginger, Wendy, and I walked the steep and windy streets of downtown Golden, passing the Chocolate Shoppe, the antique clocktower, and the theater. Dusk was falling, and one by one, the vintage lampposts that lined the narrow walkways flickered on.

We stopped in front of the Wine Jug before saying goodbye.

"Call me first thing," Ginger said, pushing open the door to the bar.

Wendy followed her in, but not before turning around and mouthing to me, "Call me first!"

I waved at them and then proceeded up the hill toward Jason's apartment. It was strange that he and I hadn't spoken all day, but maybe it was because he had a surprise in store for me . . .

Like a proposal.

I pushed the thought out of my mind. No need to go overboard with anticipation. If the time was right, Jason would know.

I'd been married before, but only for a short time. We'd both been straight out of high school and considered it a *starter* marriage. At least that's what everyone else called it, I think partly to make me feel better. Being a divorcée at twenty-one is not exactly what a girl dreams about, and it still broke my heart to think about how quickly it all fell apart for us. But things were different now.

This time around it'd be forever.

I turned the corner on Jason's street and climbed the rickety staircase to his apartment. In real estate lingo, they'd call the staircase *original*, but in reality it was one board shy of a full disaster.

I pressed the doorbell, waiting for Jason to answer. After a moment, the door flew open and my boyfriend appeared. There was stubble on his normally clean-shaven cheeks, his shirt was wrinkled, and he looked like he hadn't slept in twenty-four hours.

Ah! My computer genius.

I pressed my lips to his. "What's going on, Jason? You're a mess. Did I wake you?"

He dragged a hand across his blond hair. "No, um, I've been working. You know, I'm focusing on that promotion, so I was . . ." He shrugged his shoulders. "Did we have plans for tonight?"

"Yeah." My heart sank. He'd forgotten our date altogether. So much for a proposal. "I thought we were going to have dinner."

"Oh." He looked befuddled. "Um." He scratched his head. "I think I've got a box of pasta somewhere. You want to have spaghetti and sauce?"

"Hmm. Spaghetti and sauce sounds appetizing," I teased, poking him in the ribs, but he looked more offended than happy.

"Come on in," he said.

I followed him into his apartment. There were papers strewn across his coffee table, and his laptop was open and buzzing.

Jason did a little a jig and rotated his body so that it blocked my view of his screen. He seemed a little jittery.

Why was he acting so strange?

"Are you even hungry?" I asked.

"I could eat," he answered. "You know, I can always eat."

He padded over to the kitchen and waited for me to follow. He pulled open the refrigerator door. There was a half-full bottle of Chardonnay and a carton of eggs. Aside from that, the refrigerator was empty.

"I cleaned out the fridge earlier," he said.

"Do you want to go out to eat?"

"Out?" He suddenly looked ashen. "Uh, you know, I'm working on this project. I don't think I have time to go out. I'll miss my deadline."

"Well, I could fry a couple eggs for us," I said, ignoring the unsettled feeling creeping into my heart.

He rocked from his toes to his heels and then back again. "If you're hungry, that's fine. Or we could order takeout."

Jason was always ordering takeout, the ultimate bachelor. I figured one day when we were married, I'd show him what a regular Martha Stewart I was. I could cook with the best of them. I opened the small cupboard that made up his pantry.

"Let's see if I can find some beans and salsa or something. I'm sure I can make something yummy out of those eggs."

"No, don't bother. It's kind of a hassle to cook." He pulled out the bottle of Chardonnay and poured a glass for me.

"It's only a hassle to cook if you're not hungry," I said.

"I am hungry," he admitted.

"Well, then I'll make something." I rummaged a bit more through his cupboard and came up empty-handed. "If you had some chorizo and peppers, I could make you *Huevos a la Flamenca*."

"I love it when you talk sexy to me," he said, pouring himself a glass of Chardonnay.

I socked him in the shoulder. "It's not sexy, it's Spanish."

"Same thing."

"I guess we'll have to settle for fried eggs. You do have oil, don't you?" I asked.

He pinched the bridge of his nose as if the mere thought of groceries or anything to do with cooking gave him a migraine. "I dunno."

"It's okay. I can poach the eggs." I grabbed a pot and filled it with water as I brought him up to speed on the success of the sale and the overall events of the day. I ended with telling him that Dale Meyers was making life a living hell for the Living History Day.

Jason sipped his wine, then groaned. "Dale's a nightmare. He's making my life miserable too."

"How's that?" I asked.

Jason looked like his thoughts were a million miles away, then he said suddenly, "I've been so busy I probably haven't even told you yet, but my department head got transferred and now I report directly to Dale. It's him who's going to decide if I get promoted or not."

"Oh, Dale's not so bad. I thought you guys got along. Wasn't he the one who hired you?"

Jason was a computer engineer who did his best work uninterrupted. It was sheer misery for him to go into an office and meet with the business team, but once he and Dale met, Dale had arranged for Jason to telecommute, and Jason hadn't stepped foot into the Sacramento branch in ages.

Jason paled. "Yeah. Seems like a long time ago, though. A lot's changed." He suddenly looked depressed.

"Why don't you go work on your project while I fix the eggs?" I suggested.

His eyes lit up. "Oh . . . you don't mind?"

"I'll call you when dinner is ready." I kissed his cheek.

He kissed me back, saying, "You're the best," then disappeared to the front room where his laptop beckoned.

I proceeded to fuss about the kitchen and wipe down the counters with a paper towel. When I went to toss the paper towel, I noticed his garbage was full.

If things went according to plan, soon this would be *our* garbage! Our *New York* garbage!

Oh, who cared if Jason was busy with work tonight. Soon we'd be married. Of that I was sure.

I tied the kitchen garbage bag up and headed down the back steps where the larger trash bins for his apartment were kept: a black one for refuse, a green one for compost, and a blue bin for recycling. All the bins were stationed along the alley next to his apartment building. There was a little trail of dark droplets along the alley that lined up right to the black garbage bin.

Yuk, someone must have had a leaky bag.

I popped open the lid of the trash can and spied a man's shoe.

The shoe might as well have been connected to an electrical current, because it gave me a shock of unmeasured proportions.

What I'd considered to be garbage refuse alongside the trash can I now realized were droplets of blood.

Oh no!

What was a bloody shoe doing in Jason's trash can?

I dropped the kitchen trash bag in the alley and studied the shoe a moment, a thousand thoughts zinging through my head. I grabbed a nearby stick and prodded at the shoe. When I moved it, blood oozed out.

A chill zipped down my spine.

Whose shoe was this?

How did it get here, and why?

Suddenly, a loud bang echoed down the street and the thought struck me that I might be in danger. I slammed down the lid and raced back up the stairs to Jason's apartment.

"Jason," I screamed as I pushed open his apartment door.

He appeared at me side immediately and grabbed my arms. "What's going on? What's wrong?"

I was shaking uncontrollably, adrenaline coursing through my veins. "I went to take down your garbage . . . I . . . there's a . . . and some blood . . . I . . ."

"What? Slow down, Frannie. Calm down." He hugged me to him, the warmth emanating from his body soothing me as I took a deep breath.

"I found a bloody shoe in your garbage can," I mumbled into his chest.

He pulled away from me and looked me in the face. "You found some blood in my garbage can? It's probably from the ground beef I tossed yesterday."

"A shoe. A bloody shoe."

I must not have been making any sense, because he blinked at me, then shook his head.

"Why don't you have a seat, Frannie? Did you fall on the stairs and lose your shoe?"

"No, not *my* shoe!" I sat on his couch and stuck out my Jimmy Choo clad feet. "Someone else's shoe. A man's shoe."

He shrugged. "I don't know. Maybe someone threw away an old shoe."

"It looked new."

He sighed. "Babe—"

"And there was blood on it!"

He waved a hand at me, dismissing my fear. "I told you I cleaned out the fridge earlier. I threw out some ground beef. Probably the blood from that dripped on it or something. Look, I have to get this project done. Why don't you just chill a bit? Have some more wine and relax."

"No! You have to go see. What if there's somebody skulking around downstairs!"

He made a face.

I felt like an idiot. He had work to do, and here I was probably overreacting. Suddenly, my fear was gone, but I still needed to be sure of what I'd seen.

He sat down on the couch and pulled me to him, embracing me. "Babe, you know this promotion is important, right? It's the way we get out of this town and to the Big Apple."

"I know."

He pressed his lips to mine. "You do still want to go with me, right?"

"Of course."

"Will you feel better if I go and check out the bloody shoe?"

I laughed. "You're making it sound like a stupid joke. Remember the one about the bloody finger?"

He frowned.

I rolled my eyes. "It's the one where the girl is alone and she gets the call." I made my voice low. "This is the bloody finger . . . and I'm one block away."

He shook his head. "It sounds like a pretty bad joke."

"It is," I agreed. "The girl gets the call three times and gets more scared each time, and then a guy with a small cut on his finger arrives on her doorstep and asks for a Band-Aid."

Jason buried his head in his hands. "Worst. Joke. Ever."

"I know. It's Ginger's favorite, and she's probably told it a million times since we were kids. Every Halloween especially."

Jason rose from the couch. "Okay, I'll check it out." He made his voice low and dramatic. "The bloody shoe."

He left the apartment, and I paced.

Why was there a bloody shoe in his garbage can? I walked to the front window of the apartment and looked out into the dark street. No one seemed to be around. Certainly no one stalking the building or anything else.

I grabbed my phone and sent a group message to Ginger and Wendy:

NO PROPOSAL YET BUT FOUND SOMETHING STRANGE IN THE TRASH.

Wendy texted back first.

A RECEIPT FROM A FINE JEWELER?

Ginger texted.

A USED NAPKIN FROM THE WINE JUG WITH SOME FLOOZY'S NUMBER?

Before I could reply, Jason came back into the room. "There's no shoe in the garbage, Frannie."

"What? It's gone?"

He shrugged. "I guess so. Now we have the case of the missing shoe."

How could it be gone?

"Are you sure you looked in the garbage can? The black one. It was inside, not on top."

"Yeah, I looked inside. You left my garbage bag in the alley, by the way, and Terrance's cat was already clawing it."

Terrance was Jason's downstairs neighbor.

"Anyway," Jason continued. "Since when do you take out my trash?"

I shrugged, poured the last few drops of Chardonnay into my glass, and shook the bottle, hoping for more. I didn't want to confess that I'd been fantasizing about domesticity, so instead I said, "I was bored."

He crossed his arms. "Sorry I can't entertain you, babe, but you know—"

"I know. The promotion."

He wrapped his arms around my waist and pulled me close to him. "One more week and everything will be different. I promise," he whispered into my ear.

I pressed my cheek against his, the stubble of his beard scratching my skin.

"Why don't you go meet up with Ginger and Wendy? I won't be offended," he said.

"No! I'm not going to leave you alone on a Saturday night!"

He laughed. "Babe. I got my work. I feel like I'm the one leaving you alone. I'll walk you to the Wine Jug."

"You don't have to walk me."

"Are you kidding? I gotta make sure you leave." He chuckled at his joke, but it left me feeling unsettled.

CHAPTER THREE

I screamed as someone grabbed me from behind.

The light in the Wine Jug was nonexistent. Okay, you could see, but barely. I always did better after my eyes had a chance to adjust, but Ginger and Wendy tackled me before that happened.

Ginger giggled. "What are you so skittish about?" she shouted over the band, *Oro Ignited*, which was playing on the small stage in the corner of the bar.

Wendy dragged me to their table and poured me a glass of a local white Zinfandel. The golden hills of California were fast becoming a mecca for small wineries that couldn't afford the high real estate prices in Napa and Sonoma counties. It seemed that every day a new tasting room was popping up, and we were the happy beneficiaries.

The wine was a bit too sweet for my taste, but it was cold, and I wasn't in a complaining mood.

"I found a bloody shoe in Jason's trash."

Ginger frowned. "Was it an old shoe or what? What do you mean bloody?"

"It was a man's shoe. New shoe. Expensive. It looked like there were drops of blood on it. I told Jason about it, and when he went to check it out, it was gone."

Wendy refilled her wine glass. "Who cares about an old shoe? What happened with Jason? Did he pop the question or what?"

I shook my head, suddenly feeling self-conscious.

Ginger reached for my hand. "It's going to happen, honey. Be patient."

I nodded, trying to hide the disappointment that was surging in my body. I swallowed hard, and before tears could come, I decided to change the subject back to safe territory. "The whole shoe thing is pretty weird, huh? I can't believe Jason didn't find it. I have to go look again myself," I said over the music. Suddenly, the band took a break and I found myself still yelling, "Will you come with me?"

My face flushed as all eyes turned toward me. I smiled at the neighboring tables and then sipped my Zinfandel.

The crowd got noisy again, and Wendy leaned in. "You mean go back to Jason's and poke around his trash? No way!"

Ginger flashed me look that I interpreted as she'd go with me later when we dropped off Wendy. I nodded at her, and she winked at me conspiratorially.

Wendy was too delicate to go digging in someone's trash. Even if that someone was my intended, or soon-to-be intended.

"Come on, you're good at digging," I teased her.

"Gold digging maybe." She smiled and batted her false eyelashes at me.

"Or digging for gossip," Ginger added. "She's great at that."

"A girl has got to have special talents in life," Wendy said.

I grabbed a couple of peanuts from the bowl in the center of the table and a strange sensation tingled through me.

What if Jason was in danger?

Ben, the lead singer of *Oro Ignited* and friend to everyone in town, sauntered over to us. "Evening, ladies. Evening, Frannie." He flashed me a strange, shy look that I couldn't interpret, then turned his attention to Ginger. "I heard your jewelry designs are the hottest fad in town." He took an empty chair from nearby, spun it around, and seated himself at our table with his arms and chest resting on the back of the chair.

Ginger grinned as wide as the Cheshire cat. "Who, pray tell, told you that?"

"My Aunt Jeannie was at the sale today. She brought a flashy pendant, and now my mother is scheming to steal it . . . I mean, borrow it from her."

While Ginger made small talk with Ben, Wendy leaned over to me. "So, what's up? Why do you think Jason didn't propose tonight?"

Her question poked at a sensitive part of my heart, and I suddenly felt hollowed out. I would have much preferred to dwell on the mystery of the bloody shoe than the mystery of the missed proposal.

I'd been so sure. All signs pointed to go, and yet . . .

I shrugged and felt my eyes start to fill.

Wendy grabbed my hand. "Oh, honey! Come on." She pulled me to my feet and led me to the ladies' room. Under the fluorescent lights, I looked like the wreck of the Hesperus.

"No wonder he didn't propose! Look at me!" I yelped.

Wendy laughed and smoothed down my hair. "You be quiet. You look fine."

While Ginger had always been my closest girlfriend and had nursed me through my shares of broken hearts, Wendy was a more recent addition in my life. Being that she was married to my brother and we worked together on a daily basis at The Nugget, I was finally starting to feel like I could confide in her.

I collapsed onto the chaise in the ladies' room and sighed. "I'm not giving up. I'm still sure he's the one, but he's under a lot of pressure is all. I think next week, after he gets the promotion . . ."

Wendy ran some tap water and wet a paper towel. She quirked a brow at me as she pressed the towel to the back of my neck. "You can have anyone in town, darling. I don't want you to settle."

I frowned. "I'm not settling! I love Jason."

She nodded. "Of course you do. What about Ben? Have you noticed the way he looks at you?"

I felt a surge of defensiveness. "I love Jason. He's the one."

She dabbed delicately at her lips. "Right. Ben and I were talking earlier. He and I made a deal."

"What about?" I studied Wendy's reflection in the mirror,

wondering what was coming next. Ben had been best friends with my first husband, but they'd parted ways more or less about the time of our divorce.

"He wants me to use my power of influence with Dale Myers to get his band back on the main stage for Living History Day."

I snorted. "What power of influence?"

Wendy laughed. "Well, I am in charge of all the costumes. Don't you think the threat of having everyone dance around naked is substantial?"

We giggled. The kind of infectious, delirious laughter bubbling through us after a stressful day was enough for us to slump together and wipe the tears dry.

Taking advantage of her good mood, I said, "Come with me to have a look in Jason's garbage can."

Wendy scrunched up her nose. "I told you. I'm not digging through someone's garbage."

"You don't have to dig through his garbage. I just want to see if the shoe is there." She looked unconvinced, but I laced an arm through hers and pulled her out of the ladies' room. "What are sisters-in-law for anyway?"

"Not this!" she protested, but she didn't untangle her arm from mine.

"I won't tell," I urged.

She snickered. "Your brother would die if he knew I was digging through someone's trash."

"I know, I know. You're a gold digger, not a trash digger," I teased.

She pinched my arm. "Shut it, sister."

I laughed, but she only pinched harder until I said, "Ouch! Okay, okay, I take it back, humorless."

Back at our table, the entire band had joined Ginger for cocktails. She was flirting outrageously with all of them, sitting on someone's lap while another guy rubbed her feet. I knew I'd never be able to convince her to leave with us. Instead, I wiggled my fingers at her in farewell. She made a phone receiver out of her hand and gestured that she'd call me later.

Wendy and I exited the Wine Jug, the cool night air a reprieve from the stifling atmosphere of the bar. We walked down the streets of Golden arm in arm, Wendy chatting about the costumes she was finalizing.

Even though I tried to focus on her chatter, my mind was on the bloody shoe. When we turned the corner to Jason's block, a chill crept up my spine. What exactly was I going to do with the shoe if I found it?

We entered the alley, and a cat hissed at us, then ran off.

A black cat no less.

Wendy screeched, "Bad luck!"

I poked her in the ribs. "Don't worry about that. It's the neighbor's cat." I said it to calm her down, but the truth was I was superstitious too.

The alley was curiously clean. There were no drops of blood like before. It was as if someone had scrubbed the concrete clean.

I flipped open the lid of the black garbage can.

There was no shoe. There wasn't anything, not even garbage.

"How weird! It was here," I said to Wendy.

"Where?" she asked.

"The place is spotless. Garbage pickup isn't until Monday," I said.

"Somebody must have picked it up," she answered.

I looked through the other bins quickly. The recycling and compost bins were half-full and seemed the same as before. "It doesn't make any sense. Does it?"

"No," she said. "It doesn't make sense that you would drag me out here to look at an empty trash can."

I poked her shoulder for her to be quiet, but she was just getting started.

"It's like the time you hauled me over to the Dress Stop to rummage through the sales bins when the sale was already over. Do you remember? Or the time—"

I pulled out my phone and quickly dialed Jason, glaring at Wendy and shushing her as I left a voicemail for Jason.

"He didn't answer," I said. "I'm going to go up and see if he's okay."

Wendy flashed me a look of concern. "Why wouldn't he be okay?"

"I don't know. I'm sure he's okay. That's not what I meant. I guess I'm just freaked out."

She shrugged. "I know you were hoping for a proposal, sweetheart, but sometimes the men, they keep us waiting. Give him some space. Do you know how long it took your brother to propose?"

I wasn't about to get into this conversation with Wendy again, so I said, "Speaking of which, George is probably back from the mine and wondering where you are."

"Right. I'd better go." Wendy wrapped her arms around me and gave me a squeeze. "Walk me to Pine?"

Pine Street was only a short way down the street, and from there we'd head in different directions. We walked in silence, then said goodbye at the intersection. I knew she'd asked me to walk her this way so that she could ensure I'd head home instead of going back to Jason's.

I watched her leave, and when she rounded the next corner, I doubled back toward Jason's apartment. It wasn't worth discussing with Wendy. She didn't understand that I needed to see him again.

I rounded the corner and sat on the steps of his apartment house and called his cell again.

No answer.

He was probably working, and it would be pushy of me to intrude. After all, I'd already called him twice. Still, the matter of the garbage being whisked away was bothering me. What if something had happened to him?

No, I was being ridiculous.

I fidgeted on the stairs, not knowing whether to go up or not. I imagined Jason surprising me at the top of the stairs with a ring. Although he had been rather standoffish tonight, could it be he had a black velvet box hidden somewhere in his apartment and was waiting for the right time to ask me?

He was probably waiting for his promotion. Maybe he'd surprise me with the news of the promotion and then pop the question. Yes, that's probably how it'd go down. Jason would make reservations at the local chophouse for Friday night. That seemed fancy enough. It wasn't New York City fine dining, but at least they had white tablecloths.

Then Living History Day on Saturday; it could be my going away party from Golden. All my friends would be there, and maybe *Oro Ignited* would play after all. I'd be able to say goodbye to everybody in style with a big fat diamond on my hand.

Oh, where was Jason?

I dialed his number again.

No answer.

Forget it. I climbed the steps to his apartment and knocked at the door. "Jason?"

Silence.

He's probably wrapped up in his work.

Still. I had to at least see him one final time before heading home.

My forgetful computer genius kept an extra key under his mat. It seemed that all he could keep track of were formulas and advanced algorithms. Forget about keys and wallets. I unearthed the key, stuck it in the door, and slowly pushed it open.

I peeked my head in. "Honey."

No answer.

I tiptoed into the apartment. It was eerily quiet.

"Jason?"

Still no response.

I walked to the living room; his laptop was still aglow.

Where was he?

He'd probably gone out to get something to eat. Maybe he was at *The Spoon*, our local burger joint, enjoying a greasy cheeseburger and all the fries he could stuff into his face.

I turned on my heel and headed toward his bedroom, still calling out to no avail, "Jason?"

Before I could push open the door to his bedroom, my phone buzzed. Jason's face illuminated the screen. "Hello?" I said into the phone.

"Frannie, where are you?" Jason asked.

"Where are *you*?" I asked.

"I'm at the Wine Jug looking for you."

"Oh! I came back to your place. I was worried about you," I said.

"My place?"

Was I imagining it, or was there a tone of panic in his voice?

"Yeah. I used your key from under the mat. I got worried about—"

"Worried? Uh . . . stay there! I'll be right back," he said.

"Okay."

"Sit on the couch in the living room. I'm coming right now," he said.

"Alright, honey, no problem." The cell phone reception started to get spotty, our connection sputtering and cracking. "I'll see you in a minute," I said, ready to hang up.

"Wait for me in the living room," he said again.

"Right," I agreed.

"My bedroom's a mess," he added by way of explanation.

"Don't worry about that," I said.

Why was he all nervous and panicked? Was he hiding something in there? A black velvet box, perhaps?

We hung up, and I couldn't resist. I pressed my palm against the door to his bedroom and pushed it open.

The room was not messy at all. In fact, it was the opposite of messy. It was nearly empty.

The bed was made and a few file boxes were sitting between the closet and his nightstand, as if he'd been packing.

That was strange.

My stomach flip-flopped, an odd feeling spreading from my torso into my throat. Certainly he was planning on proposing, he was just packing up getting ready for our move to New York. That had to be right. He was packed up to move with me . . . *with* me, not without me.

Right?

I carelessly opened one of his dressers. It was empty—no socks, underwear, or small velvet box.

No!

There had to be a mistake. Jason wasn't going to leave without proposing. He was *going* to propose; we were moving to New York *together*. I knew that.

I slid open the mirrored door of his closet. Two dark suits hung side by side like lost, forgotten soldiers. The rest of his closet was packed up.

I swallowed the dread bubbling up inside my throat.

He was going to leave!

He was leaving me in Golden. He was taking off to New York after the promotion on his own. He hadn't said anything to me about packing.

A mixture of sorrow and rage boiled inside me. I kicked the trunk by the end of bed.

Was the trunk empty too?

Without hesitation, I yanked open the lid. An unexpected sight burned my eyes, and a bloodcurdling scream escaped my throat, leaving me woozy and aghast. Inside the trunk was the shoeless body of Dale Meyer.

CHAPTER FOUR

*T*he dead body at my feet both shocked and stunned me. Unthinking, I slammed down the lid of the trunk.

Oh my!

What is Dale's body doing in Jason's bedroom?

I fumbled for my cell phone and dialed 911. As the operator answered, I heard the key in Jason's front door lock.

"A dead body," I mumbled into the phone.

I heard Jason call me. "Babe? What's going on?"

Footsteps down the hallway; the operator speaking at the same time.

"A dead body?" she asked. "What's your location, ma'am?"

Jason grabbed me by the shoulders. "Frannie, what's going on?"

I muttered, "Dale's dead."

The expression on Jason's face was uncomprehending. "What do you mean?" he asked.

I frantically pointed Jason toward the trunk at the foot of his bed, while giving the operator our location. She assured me help was on the way and we hung up.

Jason flipped open the trunk and howled as he spotted Dale's body.

"Were you hoping to hide this?" I asked.

Jason looked at me, shocked. "What do you mean, hide this?"

I glared at him, my blood pressure skyrocketing and my face burning with anger.

"Frannie?" Jason's voice cracked. "What are you even asking? I have no idea how his body got here!"

I wanted to believe him, of course I believe him! And at the same time, I felt dizzy.

Could it be, I'd been planning on marrying a murderer!

"You don't have to lie about it now," I said, my heart hollowed out.

"Lie about what?" he said.

"You weren't going to marry me. You were never going to propose. You were packing up to move to New York on your own. Was Dale standing in your way, not giving you the promotion you wanted, so you decided to kill him?"

Jason looked horrified and grabbed me by the arms. "Frannie, you can't think—"

I shrugged him off. "Poor Dale!" I said.

The police would be here soon, thankfully and I wouldn't have to think about it anymore. As it was, my head felt ready to explode.

My goodness, Dale brutally murdered and lying dead at the foot of Jason's bed!

This has to be a nightmare.

I staggered toward the door, but Jason grabbed me from behind. "You can't possibly think that I had anything to do with this! I didn't kill Dale!"

"Get away from me!" I screamed over the sound of rapidly approaching sirens.

Jason looked affronted. "Frannie, please! I don't know how Dale got here."

"What about the shoe?" I demanded.

"What?" he said.

"The shoe. I told you about a shoe in the alley. The garbage is gone, the shoe is gone, and there's a dead body in your room. Jason! What am I supposed to think?"

Jason clutched at his stomach. "I think I'm going to be sick," he said.

"You should be," I replied.

He looked as if I'd stabbed him, but instead of replying, he dashed toward the bathroom. Footsteps pounded down the apartment hallway, and I yanked open the front door.

I recognized the responding officer. It was Brenda, Wendy's sister.

"In the bedroom," I said.

"Frannie, are you all right?" she asked, her long hair braided in a ponytail secured under her police officer cap.

I let her embrace me. "Yes, Brenda. I'm okay. It's Dale. He's dead."

"Dale?" she asked.

"Myers, the guy who runs the Living History Day," I said.

"Where?" She looked around. Jason's apartment was tidy. There were no signs of a struggle or a fight or, heaven forbid, a murder.

Brenda walked toward the bathroom. We heard the toilet flush. Jason opened the door, looking pale and wiped out.

"It's awful," he said. "I can't explain it."

Brenda nodded toward him and proceeded to the bedroom. "Please go into the living room," she said to both of us.

Another officer—a tall man in his thirties—appeared at the front door. We pointed toward the bedroom.

Jason grabbed my hand. "Frannie, please. You have to believe me. I have no idea how Dale ended up dead."

Still stunned, adrenaline coursed through my body. I didn't know what to think, but deep down I knew my loving gentle Jason could never have killed anyone. I collapsed onto his couch and wept. "Jason, it's so awful."

"I know," he said, rubbing my back. "Please believe me, Frannie. I had nothing to do with this."

"Your stuff is all packed up," I said through tears, hating myself.

There was a man dead in Jason's room, and I was thinking about whether or not I was getting dumped?

How callous am I?

And yet, the fear of abandonment must have been strong, because I whispered, "You're going to New York without me."

Jason gripped my hand tighter. "No, Frannie. You and I are meant to be together. Please believe me. Somebody's setting me up," he said.

"Setting you up for what?" I asked.

"For Dale's murder, obviously. Somebody stuffed him in here."

"How does somebody get a dead body into your bedroom without you knowing about it?" I asked.

He shrugged and looked befuddled. "I have no idea. I only stepped out to go to The Wine Jug and to pick this up."

He pulled something from his pocket.

My heart leaped, and suddenly overwhelmed again, I buried my face in my hands as tears sprang to my eyes.

Jason cleared his throat. "This isn't how I planned it—"

"We called the crime scene team," Brenda said, emerging from the back bedroom. "They'll be arriving soon. I'm going to need to ask you both to come down to the station with me."

I nodded. "Of course."

Jason looked befuddled. "Yeah, uh, the station, right." He shrugged.

Brenda and I both looked at Jason, our eyes landing on the item in Jason's hand at the same time: a black velvet box.

My breath caught.

Oh my goodness, he'd really done it. He'd gone out and got me an engagement ring.

Jason looked awkwardly at both of us, then turned to me. "Before we go downtown, Frannie, there's something I have to ask you."

He popped open the box. A brilliant ring sparkled at me. Instead of a diamond ring, it was gold shaped in the form of a diamond—a nugget with pink and white gold swirled together on a bright yellow band. It was breathtaking. I knew instantly my brother George had designed it.

Jason dropped to his knee. "Frannie, before we go to the police station, I have to know. Will you marry me?"

CHAPTER FIVE

I slumped in one of the hard, wooden chairs in the police station lobby, staring at the white wall in front of me. In spite of the fact that it was now well after five p.m., the station buzzed with activity, making me wonder if it was always this busy at this time of night, since Golden seemed like a fairly quiet town most of the time. It was possible that all the excitement was centered around Jason and the dead man in his bedroom. I wished that the commotion could be related to someone else—anyone else!—other than my fiancé.

I scrubbed my hands over my face.

He's not your fiancé yet, remember?

This evening hadn't gone the way Jason or I would have liked. It appeared we'd both had different plans for the night, but neither of them involved a trip to the police station and murder accusations.

I glanced at the clock, sighing. It had been nearly an hour. How on earth could asking the question "Did you kill Dale Meyer and stuff him inside a trunk in your room?" take an hour? The answer was simple: no, Jason did not kill Dale Meyer.

My heart skipped a beat.

Or did he?

I squeezed my eyes shut as salty tears pricked the backs of my lids.

All I could think about was the beautiful ring he'd offered me. He'd thought out every detail of the engagement ring with me in mind. No other man on earth would have thought to choose such a thoughtful, personalized one. Jason "got" me the way no one else ever had. Everything would have been perfect if not for that bloody shoe and, of course, Dale's corpse.

There was no way that I could be in love with a murderer. There was no way that the Jason who wanted to marry me and whisk me off to an exciting new life in New York was a killer. At least this was what I'd been telling myself since our arrival at the police station.

"Frannie?"

I lifted my face from my hands to find a distraught-looking Wendy standing before me. "I came as soon as I heard. Brenda called me. Are you alright?"

I laughed mirthlessly. "My would-be fiancé is behind bars and they found a dead man in his house. I'm doing swell."

Wendy sat down next to me. "I'm so sorry, Frannie. I wish there was something I could say that would help. But at least you found out now who he really is. I mean, before you married him."

My gaze flew to Wendy's. "Jason *didn't* murder Dale. I know him, and there's no way he'd do something like that."

Wendy's expression softened into one of sympathy as she placed her hand on my arm. "Then who did? Dale *was* found in Jason's bedroom, you know."

"I know!" I responded more sharply than I intended. I took a deep breath, slumping back into my chair, throwing my hands over my face. "What on earth am I going to do?"

"Not move to New York, I guess," Wendy answered dryly.

I sighed again.

"I'm sorry, I shouldn't have said that."

"No, you shouldn't have."

"We don't know for sure they'll keep Jason here though. Let's wait to see what Brenda has to say," Wendy said.

As if on cue, the police officer appeared from around the corner. Wendy and I stood, waiting anxiously for Brenda to speak.

Wendy and I exchanged a glance. I clasped my hands behind my back in an attempt to hide their uncontrollable shaking.

Wendy's sister looked from me to Wendy and back again. "I'm sorry, Frannie, but we're going to have to keep Jason until this mess is sorted out."

My heart sank. "I understand."

Brenda placed a hand on my shoulder. "Let me know if there's anything I can do for you."

"Besides let him out?" Wendy chuckled.

Brenda nodded, her lips pressed into a grim line. "Yeah, except let him out."

"Can I see him before I go?" I pleaded.

Brenda shook her head. "I'm afraid not, they're in the middle of processing him."

I bit my lip. I knew Brenda was only doing her job, but she made it sound like Jason was an animal instead of a man.

A man I'm in love with.

I grabbed my purse and made a beeline for the door. I didn't slow down even when I heard Wendy's hurried steps. She was working hard to keep up with me in her alligator stilettos.

"Wait up, Frannie!"

I stopped when I reached my car, but only because I could feel my cell phone buzzing in my purse. I pulled it out, groaning when I saw the name on the caller ID. It was my mother, Jessica.

I loved her, of course, but she'd never been too keen on Jason, which made speaking to her at this moment less than ideal. However, I had no excuse to ignore her call.

I held a finger up to Wendy as I answered.

"Hey, Mom."

"Honey! How are you?"

"I'm fine. How are you?"

"Fine? Are you sure, Frannie? I'm beside myself! It's all over town that Jason is a murderer!"

Oh, no, here it comes.

I took a deep breath, and Wendy's brows lowered in question.

"So, you've heard." That my mother already knew about Jason

wasn't a surprise. As a caterer, she had nearly unparalleled access to the town's most recent gossip. And being a small, historic town, Golden's rumor mill was alive and well. Only this incident with Jason was far from gossip. It was all too real for my liking.

"He didn't murder Dale Meyers, alright?"

"Now, honey," my mother said. "I understand. Nobody wants to believe horrible things about people they love—"

"Mom," I interrupted before she launched into a tirade about my father.

She made a clicking sound with her tongue, a telltale sign of her annoyance, then said, "Who else could have murdered Dale? The man, may he rest in peace, was found in Jason's bedroom. It's a terrible thing."

"Yes, terrible," I said, itching to get off the phone.

"I had a bad feeling about Jason, you know. The way he whisked into town, began dating you immediately, and then wanted to pack up and head to New York City."

A mirthless laugh escaped my throat. "Just because he has ambitions and wasn't born in Golden doesn't mean he's capable of murder."

"I just don't want to see you get hurt again," Mom said.

I nodded. "I know, Mom. I have to go."

"Alright, honey. Just one more thing before you go. I know this is a horrible thing to say, but it's good we found this out about him now before things went too far."

"Talk to you later, Mom." I hung up and shoved the phone back into my bag with more force than necessary. "I wish everyone would stop saying that."

"Saying what?" Wendy asked.

"That I'm lucky I found out now that Jason is a murderer. He's not!"

Wendy tucked her arm through mine. "Let's hope you're right, Frannie. But there's nothing we can do about it right now, so what do you say we get you home? We've all had enough excitement for one day."

CHAPTER SIX

*T*he day after Jason was arrested, I arrived at The Nugget just after nine a.m. The whole way to the shop I'd told myself to go about my day as if everything were normal. The trouble was that *nothing* was normal. I was trapped in a nightmare from which I couldn't wake up, no matter how hard I tried.

I tried to focus on the gold nuggets before me as I polished and arranged them in their glass cases. But every nugget that I looked at reminded me of the exquisite engagement ring that had almost been mine and now might not ever be. Unless I wanted to be married to a jailbird, that is.

When he'd finally asked me last night, I told him to ask him me again when this was all over.

My poor Jason. I wanted nothing more than to free him from these awful accusations and say yes with all my heart.

I slammed the sliding door to one of the cases shut, but it did nothing to quell my frustration. I was about to retreat into the back room, intent on asking Dad to tend the front since I was in no mood to deal with customers, when the bell over the front door jingled. It was Ben.

"Oh, hey, Ben. What brings you in today?"

The band leader shifted his weight, folding his arms across his chest, his eyes grazing the glass case before us. "I just thought I'd swing by. To…"

"Offer your condolences?" I remarked dryly.

Ben paused, uncertain for a moment, before nodding.

Why does he always have to act so awkward around me?

Ben cleared his throat. "That's a tough deal. I feel sorry for you since you two were…"

"Dating," I said, finishing for him once more. I forced a smile. "Yes, well, not much we can do about it. What's done is done, isn't it? Anyway, how are things with *Oro Ignited*?" I'd never been particularly fond of the music Ben's band played, but I would do anything to get off the subject of murder charges.

Ben shook his head. "Not too good. I guess you heard that Dale cancelled the band just before he, you know, died."

"Yeah, Wendy told me. Sorry about that."

"I wasn't too happy about it," Ben admitted. "I would never have wished Dale dead though."

"Of course not." I opened the glass case's door again, rearranging a few nuggets, though they didn't need it. I wished that Ben would go on his way. All this talk about Dale was making me nauseous.

"I just hired a new guitar player and backup singer for the band," Ben went on.

"Oh? Who is it?" I sounded disinterested even to my own ears, but it was the best I could do.

"His name is Graphite."

I shut the case once more, a smile coming to my lips in spite of my dejected state. "Graphite? Are you serious? He must be trying to suck up to the mining community of Golden by choosing a name like that."

"He already had the name when he arrived," Ben said. "His real name is Eugene, so Graphite is better…"

I chuckled. "Yeah, I guess so."

Ben smiled in the same tentative way he always did when he talked to me. "I know I'm talking to an expert here. Was graphite a good substance for him to choose? Is it 'cool'?"

I shook my head. "Don't tell my dad; he'll hate it. Graphite is the new gold rush. It's one of the hottest commodities on the market."

Ben's eyes widened. "Seriously? I thought pencils were old-school."

I chuckled. "It's not just for pencil lead anymore. They're using it for batteries."

"Ah," Ben said, shrugging. "Anyway, Eugene/Graphite was really bummed about the band being kicked out of the Living History Day festivities. He has big plans for himself, and having his first appearance with the group cancelled ticked him off pretty good."

"Dale Meyers made the planning difficult this year, that's for sure."

An awkward silence elapsed then. I could only hope that remaining silent would make it so awkward that Ben would go away. I didn't want to talk about Living History Day or Dale Meyers or Jason or murder anymore.

"Well, I guess I'll be going," Ben said.

Mission accomplished.

I forced a smile. "Thanks for stopping in. I'll see you around."

Ben gave me that same shy look again before leaving.

I took a deep breath once the door had closed behind him, dropping down into the folding chair behind the glass display case. I fully intended to give in to my self-pity over this drastic change of events in my life when the door opened again. This time it was Wendy and Ginger who entered. At least I didn't have to pretend with them.

"Hey, girls."

Ginger came forward immediately to grasp my hands. "Are you doing okay, Frannie?"

"Honestly, not really." I pulled my hands from her grasp, massaging my forehead with my fingertips, hoping to stave off the pounding headache developing. "I have to figure out what happened to Dale Meyers. All I've heard since last night is his name, and I'm sick of it." I exhaled. "I know the police know what they're doing and that I shouldn't be meddling but . . . I just want Jason to be cleared. The police seem dead set on keeping Jason locked up like a criminal until he's proven innocent."

Ginger and Wendy exchanged a glance.

"I can't stand by and do nothing!" I said.

Ginger fixed her eyes on me, her expression determined. "I'll help you find out who did it, Frannie. You can count on me."

I looked to Wendy. "Wendy?"

My sister-in-law appeared as unenthused by the suggestion of investigating a murder as she had about digging in the dumpster. "You're right about the police being fully capable of handling this. But I understand your need to help Jason." She paused for a moment before nodding. "Where do we start?"

"Where do all detectives start?" I said, throwing up my hands. "The suspect list."

"Do you have one?" Ginger asked.

I stood, beginning to pace. I needed to release my nerves somehow. "No, not exactly. But if we're going to get one, we need clues. Where would those clues be?"

"At the crime scene?" Wendy ventured cautiously.

I snapped, pointing at her. "Exactly. We need to go back to Jason's apartment."

Though Wendy still looked wary, she nodded. "Alright. Now?"

I nodded. "No time like the present. Ginger, are you in? Ginger?"

Ginger had become distracted with a text message on her cell phone. A moony smile played around her lips.

"Ginger?"

She looked up. "Oh, sorry, I wasn't paying attention. What did you ask?"

"Jason's apartment. Are you coming with us to investigate?"

Ginger looked back down at her phone. "I can't. I . . . uh . . . just got invited on a date."

"Really?" Wendy said. "Who with?"

"Graphite, the new member of Ben's band. Do you remember him from the Wine Jug the other night? Gosh, he's dreamy . . ."

"Yeah," Wendy replied, tossing me a wary glance. "Dreamy guitar players. That's your type alright."

Wendy's sarcasm was clearly lost on Ginger.

"You two will tell me what you find, right?" she said, inching toward the door. "I'll catch you later."

I turned to Wendy once we were alone. "I guess it's you and me then. Come on, then. Let's get to the bottom of this."

CHAPTER SEVEN

The area outside of Jason's apartment was crawling with police personnel and looky-loos alike.

"Biggest excitement Golden has seen in years," Wendy remarked. "Bigger than the time Mrs. DeLeon's prize geranium beds were decimated by Mrs. Harvey's grandson's puppy. I couldn't believe how many people stopped what they were doing to watch that showdown. Took Brenda twenty minutes to break the two women up."

"Yeah, it's exactly like that," I snapped a little more sharply than I intended. "Except this time someone wound up dead."

Wendy sobered. "You're right, Frannie. Don't worry, the police will get to the bottom of this."

Yeah, that's what I'm afraid of. If they find Jason at the bottom of it, what then?

"How are we going to get inside?" Wendy asked. "There's crime tape up and everything. I don't think we'll be able to just waltz right in."

I sent Wendy a smug look. "What's the use of having a sister in law enforcement if not to work in our favor in times such as this?"

A crack of sarcastic laughter bubbled from Wendy's throat. "Since we've had so many 'times like this.'"

My gaze swept the landscape once more. Once I located Brenda, I nodded toward her. "Come on, Wendy, there's no harm in trying. All you have to do is talk to your sister."

Before Wendy could answer, Mrs. Jeffries, who'd stationed herself as close to the caution tape as humanly possible, scurried over.

I narrowly resisted the urge to roll my eyes in exasperation when I noticed the binoculars hanging around her neck. She was breathless with excitement as she joined Wendy and me.

"Can you believe all this? Right here in Golden!"

"Thrilling," I responded.

"That Dale Meyers really had it coming to him," Mrs. Jeffries said. "But *this*!"

"He annoyed people," I agreed. "But I don't think that's an excuse to murder him. And besides, Jason had no reason to. So, it wasn't him."

Mrs. Jeffries pressed the binoculars against her round glasses, peering up at the window of Jason's apartment. I could see a police officer moving around inside. "You never know. Everyone seemed to have some grudge against that man."

"Everyone?" I pressed. "Including you?" I could see Wendy staring at me in my peripheral vision, but I ignored her. If I was going to get to the bottom of this, I needed to interview anyone who was willing to talk.

Mrs. Jeffries lowered the binoculars, her lips turning pouty. "He did ruin Edmond's and my chance to enchant the entire town, capturing the hearts and minds of those fortunate enough to hear us. He ruined that and Ben's chances too. The man was downright destructive to the authenticity of this town, if you ask me."

I exchanged a glance with Wendy. Her brows rose, assuring me that she was catching on.

Time to get our eyes on anyone with a reasonable motive.

"Maybe you're right," I said. "You must be really angry."

"Furious," Mrs. Jeffries answered. "But the lovely earrings you helped me purchase, Wendy, have been a consolation." With a smile, she reached up to finger the jewelry adorning her ears.

"Glad to hear it," Wendy said.

Mrs. Jeffries turned her attention back to the apartment building. "You know, I bet if I went around the side, I would have a better angle. Maybe then I could see what's going on inside. I'll catch you girls later." With that, she scurried off, binoculars raised halfway to her face as she made her way through the onlookers.

"Did you hear that? She's *really* angry at Dale Meyers," I whispered to Wendy.

"Are you saying that she's a suspect?"

"I don't see why not."

Wendy shook her head. "That's assuming a lot, Sherlock."

"We won't get any clues to convince us otherwise if we don't take a look inside Jason's apartment. Are you going to talk to your sister or not?"

Wendy rolled her eyes. "Fine. But no promises. This is an official investigation they are running, after all."

Wendy and I made our way over to Brenda, who was speaking with the detective who had just exited the apartment building. I strained to hear what they said, but their voices were too low, making their words indecipherable. No matter. I intended to work off of my own clues anyhow.

"Hey, you two," Brenda greeted when the detective went on his way, disappearing into his shiny cop car—the kind that camouflaged so well with regular cars that you didn't know they were watching you until the lights up top began flashing. "I'm surprised to see you here, Frannie. I would think you'd want some . . . distance from all this."

Wendy laughed. "Just the opposite actually."

Brenda frowned.

"What Wendy means to say is that we want to go inside and take a look around," I interjected.

Brenda looked from me to Wendy and back again. "Frannie, I can't let you tamper with our investigation. Golden might be a small town, but we need to keep things official."

"I understand." I sidled closer, lowering my voice. "But seeing as

I'm the girlfriend of the guy who rents this place, maybe you could make an exception? Strictly off the books?"

"I'll be with her, Brenda," Wendy chimed in. "I'll make sure she doesn't tamper with the evidence."

Brenda glanced toward the apartment, her lips twisting in indecision.

"Please?" I crossed my heart before raising my hand to solidify my vow. "In and out, I promise."

Brenda exhaled. "Sorry, no can do, not even for family."

Wendy grabbed my arm. "We understand. You're just doing your job."

I wrested my arm from my sister-in-law's grasp as she pulled me away from the apartment. "Hold on a second! I'm not going to be scared off that easily!" I glanced around.

"There's no way to get in without someone seeing us," Wendy pointed out. "Better just forget about it."

I was already shaking my head. "You're wrong. Did you notice how Mrs. Jeffries just vanished?"

Wendy's brow furrowed. "Yeah. So?"

Now it was my turn to drag Wendy, but this time around the side of the apartment. We were now so far off to the side that no one noticed when I slipped under the caution tape, pressing my back up against the apartment wall. Wendy did the same, only because if she lingered she'd be caught.

"What on earth do you think you're doing?"

I glanced up to see that Mrs. Jeffries had joined the crowd out front. We were good to go as long as we dashed into the apartment building when no one was looking.

"On the count of three, we're going to race into the apartment, okay?" I said. "One . . ."

"Frannie!" Wendy hissed.

"Two . . ." I waited until Brenda turned back to do more crowd control. Everyone was preoccupied; now was our chance.

"Three!"

In a flash, we dashed onto the porch and through the front door.

"Wait up. I can't climb the stairs this fast in heels," Wendy pleaded from behind me. "I can't believe we just snuck past the police! If anyone finds us in here, Frannie . . ."

"They won't as long as we hurry."

I made a beeline for Jason's unit. My heart sank when I got my first glimpse inside. The place looked every bit like the crime scene it was with areas blocked off and evidence labels marking each region of interest.

"I don't know what you expect to find that the detectives haven't," Wendy said as I began to look around.

"They don't know Jason like I do, so there might be something out of the ordinary around that they wouldn't find unusual. But I would."

Wendy pumped her fist in my direction. "Atta girl. Way to stand by your man. Just like Bonnie and Clyde."

"Would you stop it with the wisecracks and help me?" I said, my eyes grazing over the contents of Jason's nightstand. "We don't have a lot of time."

"Gee, you're tough. You must be the senior detective on this case, because judging by the way you're ordering me around, I'm clearly the rookie."

I shot Wendy a warning look.

She raised her hands in surrender. "Okay, okay. So what are we looking for exactly?"

"Anything unusual," I said. "Anything that seems out of place. Like this." I reached down to pick up a bracelet from off the ground near the end of Jason's bed. "What do you make of this?"

Wendy frowned at the bracelet. "Not Jason's?"

"Definitely not." I held it up for further inspection. The adornment was made up of braided leather, and there was a circular metal piece situated in the center for decoration. "It's unique, isn't it?"

"Sure is. Do you think whoever stuffed Dale in that trunk dropped it?"

"It's possible. But first things first; it's time to check with Jason and make sure he doesn't recognize it. We don't want to waste our time chasing this lead if it belongs to him."

Wendy saluted me, jabbing two fingers sharply out from her forehead. "Aye, aye, boss."

"We're investigating, not getting aboard a ship," I pointed out, tucking the bracelet into my sweater pocket.

"So you admit that we're playing Nancy Drew? Just call me Bess."

I rolled my eyes. "Fine, you win. Come on, Bess. Let's take a good look around in case there's anything else of interest. Then it's off to the jail once more."

CHAPTER EIGHT

took a deep breath as Wendy and I were led by Barney, a police officer I'd gone to grade school with, down the hall to the row of jail cells. I stared at the uneven shave of his hair below the rim of his hat. The back had always been like that, never cut straight.

Besides the bracelet, we hadn't found anything out of place in Jason's apartment. Yet, I would have rather been back there than at the jail. There was something so ominous about it!

My stomach tightened when I saw the pitiful barrenness of Jason's confinement. Golden always ensured that detainees in the jail were treated with kindness and humanity. But I knew that I'd never be able to erase the image of Jason behind bars like a criminal from my mind.

Let it fuel you to get this case solved, Frannie, not distract you.

"Frannie!"

The fact that Jason looked shocked that I'd visit pained me. I should have talked to him last night after they'd arrested him. He was my almost-fiancé, after all. He stepped up to the bars, getting as close to Wendy and me as he could.

"Hi, Jason."

An awkward silence ensued. It was strange not knowing what to say to the guy who had proposed marriage to me less than twenty-four hours earlier. But here I was, tongue-tied.

I cleared my throat, pulling the bracelet from my pocket. I held it out toward Jason. "Do you recognize this?"

Jason's eyes narrowed. "I've never seen it before in my life. Why?"

"Because we found it in your apartment."

Jason frowned, then suddenly his eyes lit up, and an expression of hope overtook his features. "You think it belonged to whoever did this . . . You believe I'm innocent, Frannie?"

I twisted the bracelet around my fingers. It was still hard for me to stomach that a dead guy had been found in Jason's bedroom. But I knew in my heart of heart's that Jason was no murderer. "Yes, I do."

Relief washed over Jason's features. "I don't know why anyone would frame me for something like this. I swear I know nothing. And I've never seen that bracelet before."

"I guess we could check around and see if anyone else in town recognizes it," Wendy suggested.

"Well, if this bracelet is a clue," I said, "you can be sure Wendy and I are going to follow it. And any other lead we get too."

Jason gripped the bars separating us. "You mean, you two are going to try to solve this case?"

"Well, technically, it's *Ginger*, Wendy, and I who are going to be solving it. But at the moment Ginger is a little preoccupied with the new head banger guitar boy over at the Wine Jug. So, I'm not sure she'll be much help."

Jason reached out his hand to me. His eyes were brimming with gratitude as I took it.

"Thank you."

My heart lurched at his touch, and I tightened my fingers around his. "This is a curve ball—a flaming, giant one. But we'll figure it out. I love you."

Jason's eyes welled with tears. "I love you too, Frannie."

As Wendy and I left the jail, I could only hope that I would be able to keep my promise to Jason. The fact of the matter was, I hadn't the faintest idea where to start our investigation. It looked as if I was going to have to learn the ins and outs of sleuthing on the go.

* * *

THE FOLLOWING DAY FOUND WENDY AND I SEQUESTERED IN THE BACK office of *The Nugget,* which we'd converted into investigation head-quarters.

"Sheesh," Wendy groaned, leaning back in her chair to rub her eyes. "Mrs. Jeffries can be a pill, but she was sure right about everyone having some beef with Dale. Every person he interacted with during the days leading up to his murder is spitting mad, mostly about his butchery of Living History Day."

"I know what you mean." I tapped the pencil I held against the wooden desktop. We'd been calling around for a couple of hours, and I couldn't make heads or tails of what information was important. Everyone was grumbling about Dale. But who had real incentive to murder him, I had no clue.

"I guess we have to look at who Dale *really* affected with his plans. I think Mrs. Jeffries has a huge motive. You know how passionate she and Edmond are about singing. Especially on Living History Day."

Wendy scowled. "So, we're definitely putting her on the suspect list? I don't like this. We've known Mrs. Jeffries for years."

"It doesn't matter what we like, Wendy," I said. "We have to be unbiased if we're going to get to the bottom of this. Unfortunately, since we live in a small town, that's going to be pretty hard to do. But we have to."

Wendy kicked her feet up, crossing her legs at the ankles as she rested her heels on the folding chair she'd been using as a desktop. She'd ditched her alligator heels a long time ago, and I could see the hot pink of her toenail polish beneath the sheer material of her footed nylons. "So, who else was all set to be involved in Living History Day?"

My brain was mush from trying to prove Jason's innocence, so I didn't even attempt to answer Wendy's question. I pulled my to-do list out of my purse, scanning it. Everything I'd intended to accomplish this weekend had gone by the wayside since the murder.

"Darn, I was supposed to pick up some sourdough bread from

Baker Pierre for my mom. She said she was out of toast, and she can't stand to use anything but the best. Apparently, his is the best."

"You're brilliant!" Wendy exclaimed.

I shrugged. "Not really. My mom is the one who figured out that Pierre's bread is heaven on earth."

"I'm not talking about the bread," Wendy said, waving her hands frantically at me. "I mean about Baker Pierre. You know how he always has his booth up on Living History Day? His baked goods are the center of attention for the event. I'll bet it's his biggest day of the whole year. It probably even trumps his Thanksgiving pie revenue. I wonder if Dale messed with his plans for the big day too."

Baker Pierre (honestly, I wasn't sure anyone knew his last name, as this was what he preferred to be called) had been in Golden for years. Like the Jeffries, his offerings on Living History Day had become a staple in this community. To suggest that he forfeit his place in the festivities would be an utter crime—not only to the great baker himself, but to the townsfolk who so enjoyed his baked treats.

I shrugged. "Let's give him a call then."

Wendy waited with her hands clasped in anticipation as I dialed the bakery on the office phone. I had to hide my smile at her childish excitement. No matter how reluctant she'd been at the start of this venture, she was really getting into her role as amateur detective alongside me.

The phone was picked up on the third ring.

"Hello?"

"Hello? Baker Pierre?"

"Yes, who's this?" The baker, who usually spoke with unreasonable gusto, even over the phone, sounded strangely subdued.

"This is Frannie."

"Frannie!"

I had to pull my ear away from the phone in order to avoid being deafened. There was that French zeal.

"Is your mother ready for more sourdough bread? Perhaps I can entice you into picking up a dozen cinnamon buns too? She'll fall madly in love with them after the first bite. Trust me."

"I'm sure you're right, Pierre, and I do actually need to pick up some bread for her."

"Bless you, *mon cherie*! You'll have the pick of every loaf in my bakery!"

I frowned at Wendy, who raised her hands in question. I covered the receiver to speak for her ears alone. "He sounds desperate for business. Trying frantically to make up for the money he was depending on making on Living History Day?"

Wendy's brows rose.

"I'll come pick up the bread this afternoon. Have things been busy?"

Pierre's voice was tinged with dejection. "Alas, there is no way for the good citizens of Golden to make up for the loss of revenue Pierre's Bakery will suffer without the Living History Day sales."

I sent Wendy a thumbs-up, mouthing *bingo*. "That bad, huh?"

"That bad. Even if every person in Golden came in today and made a purchase, it wouldn't make up even half of the business I get from out-of-town guests during the celebration. It's those out-of-towners who really buy me out. 'Tis a great pity."

I nodded, my mind working fast. "So, Dale Meyers made things pretty rough on you then? Did he bump you out of the proceedings just as he did Ben and his band? And the Jeffries?"

"He certainly did. Imagine, after all these years he wanted to bring in some city bakery to supply the baked goods."

"That's terrible. What did you say when he gave you the news?"

A shuffling ensued in the background. It sounded like the scraping of a chair being pushed out from the table, as if Pierre were standing to his feet. "You want to know what I did? Well, I'll tell you. I got right up in his face, see, and do you know what I said?"

My brows rose at the intensity that filled his voice. "No, what did you say?"

"I said that he couldn't do this to me. That he would be ruining me and everything I had worked for. It's not easy running the best bakery in Golden, you know!"

"The only one," I murmured.

"What?"

"Nothing, Pierre. What happened then?"

Another bout of shuffling ensued. This time it sounded as if the baker were raiding his baking pan collection. "I grabbed a cast iron pan and I raised it above my head. I told him that if he dared to tell me that I couldn't participate in Living History Day, I would be forced to show him what happens to anyone who threatens my business. I came to this country to grace America the Great with the delicacies of French pastry. He had no right to interfere with my destiny."

I put a hand over my mouth to stop the laugh that threatened to escape.

"And *bang!*"

I jumped when the clank of a pan rang in my ears. It seemed he'd been reenacting the entire encounter. Part of me wished I'd been there to see it. He was clearly putting on quite a performance.

"I whacked the counter with my cast iron pan so that he would know that I was serious. It was a warning . . . a warning that no one messes with the great Baker Pierre."

"Sounds like it was a pretty . . . heated encounter."

Wendy looked ready to pop with curiosity.

"It was," Pierre said. I heard the chair scraping the floor again as he presumably resumed his seat. "It'll make him think twice before disturbing my business again."

"But . . . " I ventured, carefully. "He's dead."

"Yes," Pierre said, his voice disinterested. "He certainly is."

Disturbed, I glanced back at Wendy. "Well, I'll let you go now, Baker Pierre. I'll come in for that bread this afternoon. I'm very sorry for the difficulty the recent weeks have brought on your business."

"Thank you. But at least now that the awful interference of Dale Meyers has been put to rest, we can all move on, yes?"

I hesitated for a moment, startled by the nonchalance of his statement given Dale Meyers was dead. "Uh, yes . . . well, goodbye, Pierre."

"So?" Wendy probed the moment I hung up.

I sat back in my chair with a sigh. "Well, Pierre definitely had cause to despise Dale."

"Then, you think he's a suspect too?"

"Unfortunately, yes." I tapped my pencil against the phone, thinking. "But there's just one thing: Mom is one of his most loyal customers. And Baker Pierre knows that Jason and I were together. I highly doubt that he would set Jason up like that, seeing as he has a standing sourdough bread arrangement with our family."

Wendy shrugged. "But people do crazy things when they are worked up. I've seen Pierre get pretty angry before." She laughed. "Remember when one of the ovens in his kitchen caught on fire the day before Christmas Eve? He came charging out of the building, waving a cast iron pan over his head and yelling. Before that, I would have never pinned him as the 'ominous' type, but he was certainly scary that day."

I hesitated for a moment. "I guess you're right."

Wendy's expression turned smug. "Now who's having trouble suspecting our good neighbors of a murder?"

I shook my head in resignation. "We knew this wasn't going to be easy. But at least we're getting somewhere."

"Right." Wendy was all girl detective again. She tucked a pen behind her ear, her eyes narrowing on the notepad in front of her, which consisted of every person Dale had spoken with leading up to his death. "So far we have Mrs. Jeffries and Baker Pierre as our prime suspects. What now?"

"We need to find out who that bracelet belongs to," I mused. "Maybe—" My words were cut short when my cell phone rang. I pulled it out of my bag.

It was my mother.

"Oh," I murmured. "It's my mom." I picked up just before it went to voicemail. "Hi, Mom."

"Hi, Frannie! How are you?"

"Well, Jason's in jail, the town is in an uproar . . . everything's great, Mom."

"Yeah, your dad tells me that things aren't looking too good for Jason," Mom said, her voice sympathetic. "I'm so sorry, honey."

"You talked to Dad?" The situation was worse that I'd thought if even my parents were discussing things with each other.

"It's just a misunderstanding," I said. "It'll be sorted out in no time. Brenda is seeing to that."

Wendy sent me a quizzical look, clearly disapproving of the fact that I completely skipped over the fact that we'd also appointed ourselves investigators in the case. She'd gone from being reluctant about the whole thing to being quite proud of our self-appointed positions in this case.

"I hope so. I truly hope so," Mom said. "And, honey, just because I don't necessarily think Jason is the right guy for you doesn't mean that I want him convicted of murder. Promise me you'll watch out for yourself. Let Brenda and the detectives handle this. Your heart is too involved for you to think clearly about it all right now."

I pursed my lips together, debating whether or not to admit that I was in the middle of ruling out suspects. After a moment, I opted against it. "Thank, Mom. I'll keep that in mind. Oh, by the way, I forgot about picking up the bread from Baker Pierre yesterday. But I can do it today."

"Thank you, honey," Mom said. "But I can do it. Without preparations for the Living History Day celebration to plan for, my schedule has opened up."

It seemed that Mom was the one regular at Living History Day whose usual plans hadn't been disrupted by Dale. At least I could knock my mom off the list of those with a motive for murder.

Thank goodness for small favors.

"Do you think that we won't have Living History Day at all this year because of Dale's death?"

"I don't know. Things are pretty uncertain. We'll have to see, my dear. I just wanted to check in and make sure that you're doing alright."

"I'm fine. I'll talk to you soon, Mom." I hung up the phone before standing. "Want some coffee?"

"Sure," Wendy said. I ignored the suspicion I heard in her tone. However, she insisted I acknowledge it when I remained silent. "'Yes, Mom, Wendy and I are investigating Dale's murder, Mom. We're going to see that justice is served and save Jason from life in prison, Mom.' Would that have really been so hard?" she asked.

After measuring coffee into the old-fashioned coffee maker that Dad refused to update, I turned to face Wendy. "It's none of her business, okay? Besides, it would only worry her. I'm glad she called though. She told me that she has time to pick up the bread from Pierre. That means that we can start showing that bracelet around and hopefully find someone who recognizes it."

"Well, hey, gang!"

Wendy and I turned to see Ginger strut through the open office door. The silly grin on her face gave her the unmistakable look of a girl in love.

"Let me guess, you just had a remarkable morning with your dreamboat and now he's off to rehearsal, leaving you sporting the afterglow," Wendy said.

"How did you guess?" Ginger collapsed dramatically into the desk chair. "Graphite is really the best. I've never met anyone like him."

Wendy and I exchanged an eye roll. I handed Wendy a cup of coffee, having no choice but to lean against the wall as I cradled my cup since Ginger had taken my seat.

"Glad you two are enjoying such bliss in the midst of the chaos," I remarked.

Ginger sat up straight, frowning. "Hey, it isn't our fault that Dale went and died."

"He didn't just keel over dead," Wendy corrected. "He was *murdered*. And you were supposed to help us with the investigation, remember?"

"Oh, yeah," Ginger responded vaguely. "How is that going?"

"Alright," I answered. "We've both been on the phone all morning."

Ginger jumped to her feet. "Great! Then that means that you'll be looking for a little relaxation this evening. How about coming over to the Wine Jug tonight? Graphite and his band are playing, and you should be there to support."

"So, it's *Graphite* and the band now," I said. "What happened to *Ben* and the band?"

Ginger waved a dismissive hand in my direction. "You just wait and see; Graphite is going to be bigger than Ben in no time. I feel bad that he'll outshine Ben so quickly after joining the band, but you can't stand in the way of another's chances, can you?"

I glanced at Wendy. By the look on her face, I could tell that we were thinking the same thing.

Nope, you can't stand in the way of anyone's chances—the way Dale Meyers did, giving countless people motive to kill him.

"Anyway, you two should come to the Wine Jug and support Graphite," Ginger said.

I took a sip of coffee before responding. "To be honest, Ginger, I don't feel any particular obligation to support him. I don't even know him."

"But tonight you can meet him," Ginger pointed out. She interlaced her fingers, putting them behind her head as she surveyed Wendy and me with a sly look. "You'll wish you knew him better when he and I get serious."

Wendy laughed. "For heaven's sake, Ginger, you only just met the man. Give it a few days at least before you decide."

Ginger shook her head vehemently. "I don't have to. I have a feeling about him. Come on, girls. I'm always there for you two. Come by tonight."

Wendy looked at me. "Since Ben has fallen on hard times thanks to Dale's final destruction of Golden, going over would be the neighborly thing to do."

I threw up my hands. "I can't fight both of you." I made it sound as if I was only going because I'd been coerced. However, in truth, spending so much time thinking about murder and which one of the townspeople I'd known my whole life could be capable of it had me worn out. I needed a break.

CHAPTER NINE

The moment Wendy and I sat down at a corner table in the Wine Jug, I knew that agreeing to come had been a mistake.

"When Ginger asked us to join her in supporting the band, I didn't realize that she was going to be *up there* with Pea Gravel."

I laughed. "It's Graphite."

Wendy rolled her eyes, taking a sip of her margarita. "Whatever. She can't seem to peel herself off of him."

I looked up at the stage. Ginger was making quite a spectacle of herself with her arms around Graphite's neck, her body pressed up against his back as he played his guitar. It was embarrassing to watch, but I couldn't help smiling. "She always was a wild one."

"I'm surprised Ben is allowing such shenanigans on his stage," Wendy said, continuing to shake her head in disapproval.

I chuckled. "Ben's never been the law-and-order type. Besides, it's not like Ginger is doing any harm."

Wendy snorted. "Yeah, only to my eyes."

The song ended then, and we applauded as the band broke up for a break. Ginger skipped immediately over to our table, hauling Graphite along behind her.

"Girls, I want you to meet the musical legend I've been telling you about. The one and only, Graphite!" Ginger opened her arms wide, wiggling her splayed fingers in a dramatic Broadway Jazz Hands display.

"Nice to meet you both." Graphite looked every bit like what one would expect of a wannabe headbanger. With the gauge earrings, spikey, punk-rocker hairstyle, and graphic tee, he looked practically naked without his electric guitar.

Wendy had become absorbed with her martini, stirring it with the orange umbrella toothpick before pinching the olive on the end off with her teeth.

"Nice to meet you too, Graphite," I said, seeing that it was up to me to ensure that we didn't come across as completely unwelcoming.

"Do you have time to sit down, Graphite?" Ginger asked, hanging on to the guitar player's arm.

"We're on break. Sure, I can sit down."

While Ginger and Graphite got situated, I issued a meaningful kick to Wendy's leg. Her eyes darted to mine in annoyance. I pursed my lips at her, nodding subtly toward Graphite.

Mind your manners, sister-in-law of mine. It's been a long couple of days, and I have no intention of picking up the slack for you tonight just because you don't like Ginger's new crush.

I sighed inwardly, drawing a row of lines through the condensation on my glass. I was beginning to doubt the wisdom of coming out tonight. But we were here, so I had little choice but to do my best at conversation.

"So, Graphite, Ginger tells us that you have big plans for your musical career."

Graphite's face lit up immediately, and he leaned forward in enthusiasm. "I definitely do. You know, I'm from Oregon. But I didn't see much for myself there. Besides, every musician needs to spend time in California if he wants to make it big!"

"And you figured Ben's band was the place to start, huh?" Wendy piped up, her voice dripping with sarcasm.

I sent her a warning look, but Graphite had either failed to notice her response or had chosen to ignore it.

"Yup," Graphite answered. "I figure you have to get in front of the public somehow. Why not do it in a town like Golden?"

"Yeah, why not?" Wendy said, her voice filled with false brightness.

I considered sending her another kick under the table, but I figured it wouldn't do any good. Wendy was set in her ways when it came to people, and she was clearly set on disliking Pea Gravel.

"You must have been pretty disappointed when Living History Day was cancelled then. It's the biggest day for performers around here."

"Since we have such an abundance of talent in this town," Wendy muttered, taking a long drink from her glass.

If I allowed Graphite to notice Wendy's cynicism, I'd likely have little chance of getting any information out of him, so I did my best to keep him engaged. "I'm sure you know that Ben and his band have been a centerpiece of the festivities for years."

Graphite shrugged. "I heard about that."

I glanced at Wendy. "You don't sound very disappointed. I would have thought you'd be looking forward to performing. It would have served as a nice debut here in Golden, don't you think?"

Graphite shrugged again before looking at Ginger. "Well, what's done is done, I guess. No use crying over spilled milk, right, Ging?"

Ginger grinned cheekily, earning a smile from her new boyfriend in return.

Graphite and Ginger remained moonily caught up in each other's eyes long enough for me to share a significant look with Wendy. Golden's newest citizen certainly appeared nonchalant about Dale Meyers's death. Maybe a little too much so? It was a strange contrast to the kind of hysteria I'd experienced from the other citizens at the mention of Dale's violent death.

The subject of Dale was abruptly discarded when Ginger launched into more detail about how great Graphite had been as head of a music troop in high school. I was amazed that she seemed to know so much about him after such a short time. Graphite had clearly succeeded in capturing her heart.

It looked as if we were to be condemned to an evening of listening to Ginger brag on her new boyfriend when Ben arrived at our table. For once, I was relieved to see him. Anything that would distract me from Graphite and Ginger's nauseating fawning was welcome.

"Hey, Ben. How's everything going?"

Ben shifted his weight, sending me a tentative smile. Wendy, whose face had lost its boredom and was now alight with mischief, bumped my shoulder, her eyes glinting with teasing.

I waved her off. "Stop it," I whispered.

Ben cleared his throat, looking as uncomfortable as always. "How did you like the performance, Frannie?"

"It was good, Ben," I said, purposefully avoiding the gaze of everyone else at the table. They were all watching us as if we were an item.

"You know," Ginger piped up, looping her arm through Graphite's as she gazed lovingly at him. I'd never seen such doe eyes in my life. "We should all hang out sometime—you, me, Frannie, and Ben. It would be perfect, don't you think? Since Frannie and I are friends and you and Ben are?"

"Thanks for the invite, but I'll have to pass on this one," Wendy interjected dryly. "I hate being the fifth wheel."

The relief I'd felt initially at Ben's arrival vanished. Spending time across the table from Ginger and Graphite in a group setting was one thing, but a double date arrangement was something else entirely. Besides, my boyfriend wasn't gone—just trapped behind bars. There was no way I was going anywhere as Ben's date.

"I'm kind of busy in the near future, but maybe," I responded evasively.

"Oh, no problem," Ben was quick to say before we all lapsed into an awkward silence once again until Ginger spoke.

"Graphite, will you let me hold your guitar? I've always wanted to hold one like yours and pretend I'm a rock star."

"You are a rock star, baby," Graphite said, flashing her a smile.

Wendy covered her face with one hand, making no attempt to hide her disgust.

The lovebirds made their way back to the stage, and Ben, who clearly had no idea how to continue the conversation because of my presence, mumbled something about doing a sound check before the band was up again.

I exhaled, shaking my head. "Ready to go, Wendy? I think we've fulfilled our nonexistent obligation to come and support the head-banging wonder."

"I don't care much for the hand banging wonder, but I sure noticed how Ben was acting tonight," Wendy remarked.

I grabbed my purse, draining my glass. "What do you mean?"

Wendy lifted one eyebrow at me. "Don't play dumb. Ben is clearly into you. The guy can't put two sentences together when you're around."

I rolled my eyes. "Yeah, well, I'm not sure what's up with that. What I do know is that Jason isn't going to get himself out of jail. Tomorrow let's meet at eight o'clock sharp at *The Nugget*. We need to come up with a game plan based on the information we gathered today."

"Just as long as we don't have to do any more investigating tonight, I'm good with that," Wendy answered when we reached the exit door of the Wine Jug. My sister-in-law glanced at her watch. "My hubby's going to be wondering where I am. *Hasta mañana.*"

I looked back to the stage where Ginger was enjoying both her moment as a rock star and the glory of Graphite's undivided attention before leaving.

I'd hoped that a trip to the Wine Jug would be rejuvenating, or at least relaxing. Instead, my mind remained in turmoil. Even after a long day of investigating (or at least doing what I *believed* to be investigating), I still didn't feel closer to finding Dale's murderer. Could be Pierre. Could be Mrs. Jeffries. Could be Susanna of the Mountains.

I couldn't help walking by Jason's apartment on my way home. What I saw when I got there made me stop in my tracks and squint into the darkness.

Speaking of Mrs. Jeffries . . .

I took a few steps closer to where she was tiptoeing over the apartment complex's front lawn.

Was she peeking into windows?.

"Mrs. Jeffries?"

Mrs. Jeffries whirled around to face me. In her hands, she clutched the same pair of binoculars she'd brought along the day the police canvassed the area. Her eyes were wide as saucers as she stared at me.

A moment passed before she pressed her hand to her generous bosom, releasing a nervous laugh.

"Heavens, Frannie, you startled me."

"Sorry?" I ventured. "Um ... what are you doing?"

Mrs. Jeffries's hands came up to adjust the absurdly ruffled collar of her dress, though she only succeeded in rumpling it further. "I was just checking around to see if the police missed anything."

I crossed my arms over my chest. "Oh? Any luck?"

Mrs. Jeffries frowned. "No. But I was thinking that maybe if I could get a look at what the neighbors are doing, I might find a clue."

I barely managed to keep a straight face. "A clue? Like what?"

"You know, someone cleaning up blood or even a murder weapon. Or better yet, talking about how to dodge discovery by the police. The walls in these old apartment buildings are thin. If you find a crack and press your ear right up against it, you can hear every word spoken on the other side."

"You're thinking it was someone in the building then, huh?" Mrs. Jeffries's methods were comical, to say the least. However, my desire to receive any insight at all was sincere in spite of it.

"It would make sense, wouldn't it? Then he—or she—could just run back to their apartment once the deed was done." Mrs. Jeffries shuddered. "I can't imagine that murderer slept too well after going through with it." Her expression became thoughtful as I waited in silence for her to continue. "There is one observation that makes me think perhaps this wasn't an inside job ..."

Everyone was getting into sleuth speech. First Wendy, now Mrs. Jeffries. It was as if the entire town were made up of detectives.

"What was your observation?" I asked.

Mrs. Jeffries glanced furtively around before motioning with two fingers for me to come closer. Once I had, she leaned in so close that I could smell the tang of her perfume.

"I saw Pierre here the other night."

I frowned. "Pierre? As in Baker Pierre?"

Mrs. Jeffries nodded vigorously. "One and the same. I saw him drive up and dump a whole load of trash into the dumpster over there." Her voice lowered even further, her words coming out as more of a hiss than a whisper. "Could have been a body in that mess of refuse."

All at once, my throat went dry. I remembered the sound of Pierre banging the cast iron pan on the countertop . . .

No! He was on our list, sure, but he would never be capable of such a thing! Would he?

I wasn't aware that the intensity building within me showed on my face until I looked back to Mrs. Jeffries to find her own tinged with panic.

"I wasn't doing anything sneaky if that's what you thought, Frannie Peterson," Mrs. Jeffries said. Her brow lowered in determination. "I'm just dying to get to the bottom of this."

"Well, we all want to know what happened," I conceded. "I guess all we can do is keep our eyes open, huh?"

"That's right, Frannie."

I cast around for something else to say, but came up short. "I guess I'll head home now. Have a good night, Mrs. Jeffries."

"Good night, Frannie."

As I made my way down the block, I turned to look back at Mrs. Jeffries before Jason's apartment would be out of sight. She was up on tiptoe with her ear pressed against the wall outside of a first-floor apartment. I shook my head. She was a little batty sometimes, but I had to admit that what Mrs. Jeffries said about Pierre had hit hard. It looked as if the baker was now, inescapably, a suspect on our list.

CHAPTER TEN

he next day, Wendy and I would have dove right back into investigating had Dad not insisted I spend some time at the front desk of *The Nugget.*

"I understand why this case is important to you," Dad said. "But the police are on it. You still have a job to do here, Frannie."

I knew that he was right. I would work my usual shift. But there was no way Dad could stop me from turning over the possibilities of the case in my mind while I worked.

Mrs. Jeffries was angry with Dale Meyers for taking away her and Edmond's chance to perform, and Pierre was clearly furious that Dale had sought to bring in a baker from out of town for Living History Day. Then there was Graphite. He hadn't seemed angry with Dale at all, though he had as much right (perhaps even more of a right) to be upset as anyone.

I need to figure out a way to get them all to look at the bracelet. Their reactions would be telling if they were to recognize it as an item they'd lost on the night of the murder

The bell over the front door jangled. Wendy stepped across the threshold, striding toward me. She wore a smart, black, button-up coat and a stylish fedora. She looked like a 1920s detective, and I wondered if her clothing had been inspired by our investigation. She plunked a to-go cup of coffee down on the counter in front of me. "So, where do we start today?"

I slid open the display case in front of me, removing the pieces that needed polishing. "I have to work today."

Over the rim of her own coffee cup, Wendy's eyes grew wide with disbelief. "Are you kidding? We can't stall now."

I glanced toward the office where Dad sat at the desk. "Dad reminded me that I have a job to do. I can't just abandon it."

Wendy's expression remained unconvinced, her hand going to her waist in annoyance.

When I was sure Dad was absorbed in his work, I leaned across the counter to speak for Wendy's ears only. "I might not be able to work on the case today, but I had an interesting run-in with Mrs. Jeffries last night."

Wendy tilted her head. "Really? Tell me."

I lowered my voice even further. "I walked by Jason's apartment, and who do you think was creeping around out front looking in windows?"

Wendy covered her mouth to quiet the crack of laughter that shot from her lips. "Are you serious? What did she say when you saw her?"

"That she's investigating, just like us."

"By looking in windows?"

I nodded. "She was thinking that she might overhear a conversation related to the crime through the thin walls."

"Wow." Wendy frowned. "She's on our suspect list though, since she was so hurt over her and Edmond's dismissal from performing on Living History Day. If she were involved in the crime, would she really be snooping around like that? It seems like it would be a waste of her time."

"Unless she's trying to clean up anything that could incriminate her," I said.

Wendy chuckled.

"Alright. You have a point," I agreed. "Maybe we can consider scratching her off the list because it seems she's keeping one of her own."

"She heard something through the apartment walls?" Wendy asked dubiously.

"No, but she did *see* something. She says that Pierre was dumping a whole load of trash into the dumpster outside of Jason's apartment the other night."

"Why would he do that?"

I shrugged. "Maybe he had something in the trash that he didn't want found in his dumpster pile at the bakery?"

Wendy sipped her coffee thoughtfully. "And you said when you talked to him, he was spitting mad at Dale. Dang, it seems that Golden's renowned pastry man bit off more than he could chew."

"We don't know for sure that this trash dump incident proves guilt," I pointed out. "But we should keep an eye on him."

"I agree. Maybe—f"

Wendy's words were cut off when the bell over the door jangled, this time admitting the snooper herself. Mrs. Jeffries waved a handkerchief at us before making her way around the store.

"Morning, Frannie. Morning, Wendy."

I half-expected to see the binoculars around her neck, but it seemed she'd made a trip without them today.

"How are you girls doing this morning?"

"Just fine, Mrs. Jeffries," I answered. "Can I help you find anything?"

"I'm just browsing." Mrs. Jeffries's gaze swept the cases as she passed them. However, the fact that she was practically moving at a canter made it impossible for her to truly study the contents. She clearly wasn't interested in gold today.

Once Mrs. Jeffries completed her unconvincing jaunt through the store, she made a beeline for Wendy and me. The moment she reached us, she began talking.

"Have you two girls heard about the most recent uproar?"

Wendy and I exchanged a confused look.

"You mean . . . Dale's murder?" I ventured.

Mrs. Jeffries waved her hands. "No, no, no. I mean that decorator from out of town."

Wendy and I continued to regard her in bewilderment.

"The one who was hired to do the setup for Living History Day."

"I thought that Mrs. DeLeon always handled the decorations," Wendy said.

"She does." Mrs. Jeffries wagged her pointer finger, her expression growing conspiratorial. "But not this year."

"Let me guess," I said. "Dale Meyers had something to do with it."

"Right. He hired an out-of-town company, and they've already started bringing all of their equipment into the downtown square."

"How did you hear about this?" I asked.

Mrs. Jeffries's eyes danced with mischief as she leaned in. "The day before Dale was found dead in Jason's apartment, I heard the two of them having it out. Mrs. DeLeon was yelling, saying that he couldn't kick her off of the decorating committee—that decorations had been her responsibility for years!"

"But that didn't stop Dale from hiring out," I said.

Mrs. Jeffries nodded. "Now that Dale is dead, the out-of-town company wants to be repaid by the town of Golden for the hours they've already invested in beginning the setup. If he hadn't hired someone from the outside, the town wouldn't be in debt right now."

Saying that Golden was now "in debt" was a leap, but I understood what she meant.

"Anyhow, before Dale kicked the bucket, I heard Mrs. DeLeon trying to convince him that it was always better to keep things local, but he wouldn't listen. She was furious when he turned her down flat."

"Must have been devastating for her," Wendy said.

Mrs. Jeffries nodded vigorously. "She stormed away so angry. She looked fit to kill."

We all knew that Mrs. Jeffries's choice words were no accident. She was trying to tell us that she'd found another suspect.

"Well, thanks for updating us on Golden's most recent plight," I said. "Was there anything you wanted me to get out of the display cases for you to look at?"

Mrs. Jeffries's surprised expression made it clear that she'd forgotten all about the merchandise. "Oh, the display cases . . . No, I don't think I'll purchase anything today. I have things to do before dark."

With that, Mrs. Jeffries bustled out of *The Nugget* as quickly as she'd marched in.

"Where do you think she's off to so fast?" Wendy asked.

"She's going to go listen in on people's conversations through the walls of Jason's apartment building. Anyone could have guessed that," I said, chuckling in amusement.

"But it's not even nine o'clock. If she's waiting until dark, why does she have to leave now?"

"She must need time to grab her binoculars."

Wendy rolled her eyes. "Right."

I tossed the rag I'd intended to use to polish the merchandise aside. "Well, we'd better get going."

Wendy frowned in confusion. "But your dad said no investigating today."

"Doesn't matter," I whispered. "This is too good to pass up. Mrs. Jeffries, Ms. Harvey, and Mrs. DeLeon are always in competition with each other, whether it's outdoing each other on Living History Day each year or buying up the best jewelry at one of Ginger's exhibitions. We need to chase this tidbit Mrs. Jeffries just gave us on Mrs. DeLeon's beef with Dale."

Wendy twisted her lips uncertainly. "I can't believe that Mrs. Jeffries would suggest that Mrs. DeLeon is a murderer though. Isn't she going a little overboard?"

I chuckled. "Sneaking around town with binoculars and peeking into people's windows at night is also going overboard in my opinion. The woman is all in. All she cares about right now is the investigation."

"I'm starting to think that a real, live murder is a busybody's dream," Wendy replied dryly. "If she's so intent on finding out who committed the murder, why does she keep passing all the clues on to us? It seems to me she'd want to keep her hunches to herself."

"You know Mrs. Jeffries—she can't keep anything to herself. You saw how she was when she came in here; she looked at the merchandise for two seconds before coming over to gossip about Mrs. DeLeon. She came in with the intention of telling us about her discovery. She's definitely being over the top about this, but I have to admit that her hunches have made sense, even if her investigation tactics don't appear particularly efficient. I say we jump on this tip about Mrs. DeLeon and talk with her now."

I waited until Dad was on the phone before grabbing my purse, motioning for Wendy to follow me out the back door.

"George is going to be pretty miffed when he finds out you skipped out on your shift."

"I think he'll be a whole lot more miffed if his daughter ends up disgraced after her intended is sent to prison," I retorted as I power walked toward Mrs. DeLeon's residence. As always, Wendy fought to keep up with me, tottering precariously on her heels as she dodged sidewalk cracks. "He'll be annoyed now, but he'll thank me later."

Mrs. DeLeon's house was a few minutes off the main drag on a dead-end street. I hadn't been in this area for a long time and had completely forgotten her elaborate front yard.

We could hear the wind chimes dangling from every direction before we even caught sight of the house. Lawn ornaments ranging from flowers to dinosaurs seemed to go on for miles alongside rows and rows of primrose, daisy, and pansy beds.

I released a low whistle. "I forgot how . . . colorful this place was."

Wendy laughed. "That's one way to put it. And just think: Dale wanted all of Golden to miss out on this caliber of decorating this year," she said, motioning to the display around us.

I swatted her arm. "Be nice. The decorations for Living History Day usually look pretty good. Mrs. DeLeon is allowed to get as crazy as she wants with her own house. This is the one place where she can fully express herself."

"You can say that again," Wendy muttered as the front door to the house opened.

Mrs. DeLeon walked out of her house with a garish, hot-pink watering can in hand. She watered the potted geraniums on the front porch for a moment before noticing us.

"Hi, girls. What are you two doing out this way?"

"Just thought we'd stop by and see how your garden is doing," I answered.

"Good one," Wendy whispered. "Go straight for the flattery."

"Well, we want her to talk, don't we?" I replied. Everyone knew that there was nothing that Mrs. DeLeon liked to talk about more than her own skills.

"That's so thoughtful of you!" Mrs. DeLeon exclaimed, motioning for us to join her on the front porch, where she proceeded to point out every new flower and plant "since our last visit." She seemed to remember when that was, though I couldn't.

A solid fifteen minutes passed before she invited us inside. Just as the busy state of the garden had stunned me after a long time without seeing it, the house managed to shock me just as much, if not more.

Mrs. DeLeon had always been fond of porcelain dolls, but the number lining the shelves seemed to be double what I remembered. I was sure she'd changed the wallpaper too. It was now a pineapple print that matched the lemon-yellow curtains. The living room furniture was white wicker that would have looked perfectly at home on the front porch.

"Would you girls like anything to drink? Pink lemonade?"

"Sure, thanks, Mrs. DeLeon," Wendy answered.

Wendy and I sat down in the wicker chairs while our hostess disappeared into the kitchen.

"She could have hidden a body here and no one would have noticed," Wendy whispered, motioning toward the doll display. "There are already so many dead-looking people around, no one would think twice about one more."

I couldn't help laughing. "I hate to say it, but you're right about that."

"Right about what?"

Wendy and I turned to find that Mrs. DeLeon had arrived back with a tray of three tall, skinny glasses of lemonade that was nearly as pink as the watering can outside. She'd always been one for outlandish color choices.

"Your doll collection," I responded, thinking fast. "We were saying that your doll collection has grown."

Mrs. DeLeon paused in passing out the lemonade glasses to admire her dolls. "It certainly has. It's a fun hobby. There was a doll show that I thought I was going to miss because of Living History

Day, but it looks like I'll be able to go now. Maybe going will take my mind off of not decorating for the festivities . . ." Mrs. DeLeon trailed off, staring down into her own glass of lemonade.

"We heard about how Dale slighted you," Wendy ventured. "Sorry about that. But you're in good company. It sounds like just about everyone was excluded from the festivities this year before Dale's . . . accident."

"That doesn't excuse it." Mrs. DeLeon sat down, taking a long drink from her glass.

"Mrs. Jeffries told us that you were pretty upset when Dale told you that you wouldn't be handling the decorations," I said.

Mrs. DeLeon pressed her lips into a stubborn line. "Well, of course I was. Wouldn't you be?"

I nodded. "Yes, I suppose so. She said you were so upset you yelled at him though."

"I wasn't the only one who argued with Dale over this." A defensive note had entered Mrs. DeLeon's voice. "I was there when Dale dropped Ben's band too. He told the band right in front of the Wine Jug that he was hiring another group. He went berserk."

"Ben went berserk?" I said. "I can't really picture that . . ."

"It wasn't Ben exactly. It was that new member he's brought on. The one with one bullet hole in each ear."

Graphite.

"You mean gauge earrings?" I clarified.

Mrs. DeLeon scowled. "They look like bullet holes to me. Why anyone would ever want to look the way that boy does, I'll never understand. Well, anyway, it was that fellow who got really angry about being dropped."

Wendy jabbed me with her elbow. "Looks like Pea Gravel can really kick the dust up."

I rolled my eyes, waiting until Wendy finished laughing at her own joke before speaking. "That's funny . . . When we talked to him about it the other night, he didn't seem particularly bothered by the setback."

Mrs. DeLeon's brows rose quizzically. "Oh, believe me, he was." She clicked her tongue, shaking her head. "Being excluded from

Living History Day is a big bummer for Ben. I happen to know that he doesn't have a lot of money, so this kind of setback has to be *huge* for him. It's disgraceful how the band handled being dropped though."

"To be fair," I retorted. "It isn't exactly Ben's fault that his newest group member blew up like a volcano. It's not like he can control the guy."

Mrs. DeLeon waved my words off. "Defend him how you will, I still view them as a group of sore losers. Sour grapes is all it is."

"Can't say I blame them," Wendy admitted.

Mrs. DeLeon lifted her hands to the ceiling in resignation. "If Dale had only listened to what I told him about the dangers of hiring from out of town, Golden wouldn't be in this fix. He should have listened."

Her words caused a shiver to shoot up my spine. I'd tried to convince myself that Baker Pierre's heated threats toward Dale had been empty, and I wanted to believe that Mrs. DeLeon's ominous comments were as well, but I couldn't quite manage to discard them as "nothing." The smug look on Mrs. DeLeon's face as she took a long drink from her lemonade glass and shrugged only deepened my wariness.

More sour grapes? There seems to be a pretty hefty bushel in Golden, and all because of Dale Meyers.

I looked back at Wendy, who quirked an eyebrow in response as she finished off her lemonade.

Which sour grapes to follow . . . that was the question.

I sipped my lemonade while Mrs. DeLeon updated us on all of the improvements she'd made on the house in the name of distracting her in the midst of her mourning.

"I just don't think I'll ever get over being excluded from Living History Day this year," she said as she escorted us out. "But at least it gives me time to redecorate."

"Yes, I'm sure you're right," I said as we stepped out onto the porch. "Thanks again for the lemonade, Mrs. DeLeon."

"Creepy dolls, ludicrously pink lemonade, and too many lawn ornaments . . . but no clues," Wendy said as we made our way back into town after leaving Mrs. DeLeon's house. "Do you think that Mrs.

Jeffries sent us in Mrs. DeLeon's direction out of spite? Or maybe to throw us off the scent of the real killer?"

"I was wondering the same," I admitted. "Mrs. DeLeon might feel like another dead end, but there is one suspect I can't get off my mind."

"Baker Pierre," Wendy guessed with a sigh.

I shrugged. "I hate to say it, but he seems to have the most convincing combination of motive and pent-up anger about the whole thing."

"And don't forget what Mrs. Jeffries said about his mysterious visits to the dumpster behind Jason's place," Wendy said.

"Exactly."

Wendy frowned. "But what about all that jazz about Graphite losing his mind over the band's expulsion from the festivities?" She bumped my elbow. "All that *jazz*? Get it? Since he's a musician?"

I laughed. "I'm pretty sure it should be 'all that rock-n-roll.' He's got gauge earrings, remember?"

Wendy shook her head. "I have to agree with Mrs. DeLeon. I don't know what Ginger sees in him."

I reached into my purse when my phone began to ring. I waved it in Wendy's direction as Ginger's name glowed on the screen. "Speak of the devil." I answered the phone, putting it on speaker as Wendy and I continued to walk.

"Hey, Ging. What's up?"

"Are you ready for some real fun?"

Wendy and I exchanged a confused glance.

"You mean more fun than we're having tracking down a murderer?" Wendy said. "I don't know if you recall, but you were actually supposed to help us with that . . ."

"Just wait," Ginger rushed on. "You're going to be ready to take a break when I let you in on what I've got planned for tonight."

"Oh no," Wendy moaned. "Don't tell me: it involves Graphite in some shape or form."

"Of course!" Ginger exclaimed. "Graphite has scoped out the coolest bar in Sacramento. He's agreed to take us all out this evening for some big city fun."

"That's super generous of him, but I don't think—"

I waved frantically at Wendy, shushing her before she could finish.

"That's nice of him," I said. "Sure, I think we can take an evening off from investigating to kick it with you guys." I ignored Wendy's glare.

"Great!" Ginger cried. "Why don't you two come over to my place around six and he'll pick us up?"

"Sounds like a plan. Bye."

Wendy attacked me the moment I hung up the phone. "Have you lost your mind? I'm not going out with Ginger and Pea Gravel. Call me a wet blanket, but I for one am not thrilled with the idea of sitting in the audience while the two of them put on their own little show again." She pretended to gag. "Their PDA is honestly *too much*."

"I couldn't agree more, but think about it," I said. "Mrs. DeLeon did say that Graphite nearly started throwing fists when Dale broke the news about the band. This could be a great opportunity to get the scoop on what happened."

An aggravated moan escaped Wendy's throat. "Do we have to?"

"Don't be so dramatic; it won't be that bad. And it could actually prove super valuable. Come on." I chuckled when she still looked unconvinced. "Take one for the team. Team Girl Detectives, right?"

Wendy exhaled. "Oh, alright. But if they start all that staring-endlessly-into-each-other's-eyes nonsense, I'm leaving."

"Fair enough."

I had to admit that I was a bit insecure about how to go about this investigation. What I did know was that I had a hunch about Graphite. I figured we couldn't lose anything from following it.

Isn't that what detectives do—go after hunches?

All I could do was follow it and find out.

CHAPTER ELEVEN

*W*endy's jaw hit the floor the moment Ginger answered her apartment door. I knew that my eyes were as big as saucers as well. The girl was more decked out than I'd ever seen her.

She'd paired a lacy, black top with a brand-new pair of jeans that featured so much bling on the back pockets, I wondered if it would hurt to sit down. She'd flat-ironed her hair before shaping it into luxurious curls. The biggest chandelier earrings I'd ever seen poked out whenever she tossed her head.

"I'm sorry, I think we have the wrong house," Wendy said, taking a few steps backward. "We're here for Ginger, not Madonna."

Ginger laughed, turning in a circle for our inspection. "What do you think?"

"I think you look like you're ready to put on a show," I answered.

Wendy swatted my shoulder. "Don't give her any ideas."

Ginger laughed again, rising up on tiptoe to look behind us, presumably in anticipation of Graphite's arrival. "The bar Graphite is taking us to is a big deal—nothing like the Wine Jug—so I doubt we'll get to go up on stage."

"Thank goodness," Wendy muttered.

Ginger bounced up and down like a child when Graphite's car pulled into the apartment's parking lot. "He's here! Come on, let's go!"

Wendy and I trailed behind her after she pushed past us, racing toward her rock star.

"I wish I hadn't agreed to this," Wendy moaned.

"Would you stop whining?" I exhaled. "I'm betting you that this is going to be worth it. I've got a feeling about Graphite . . . just trust me."

"I'll try, but it will have to be one whopping great piece of evidence for me to consider this worth my time."

"Don't worry, it will be," I said, even as I worked to convince myself of this fact.

"Well, lucky me," Graphite said as he and Wendy stood next to his car. "I get to escort three lovely ladies tonight."

"Too bad Ben couldn't come with." Ginger tore her sheep's eyes from Graphite long enough to send me a suggestive wink.

"It's really okay," I said. "I think the four of us will manage just fine. Won't we, Wendy?"

Just as she had in the bar, Wendy was doing her best to pretend that Graphite didn't even exist. Once again, Graphite didn't appear to take any offense.

Graphite tossed his arm around Ginger's shoulders. "Ben and I have sure had fun having Ginger here as a sidekick. Hope you don't feel like we stole her from you."

"No, not at all," Wendy murmured sarcastically.

"Well, let's hit the road, ladies." Graphite opened the passenger door for Ginger. "I have an exciting playlist in store for you all. The demo CD of my latest album is here, and I want you three to be the first to hear it."

"Can't wait." Wendy looked more and more annoyed by the second.

"I'm so excited to hear your songs, Graphite!" Ginger gushed as she jumped into the car while Wendy and I took the back seat. I had to situate myself carefully in order to avoid upsetting the boxes of junk at our feet. It looked as if Graphite lived in his car.

"You're so talented," Ginger fawned as Graphite popped the proof

CD into the player. "This whole town deserves to be graced with your musical abilities."

Wendy moaned, dropping her face into the palm of her hand as Graphite started the car.

Graphite grinned at Ginger, swooping one of her hands into his own. "I'll get my chance here in Golden, baby, you wait and see. Now that that old miser Dale Meyers is out of the picture, I have a feeling there are going to be lots of opportunity for the talent in this town to shine."

I looked over at Wendy to find her already looking at me with wide eyes. His words weren't threatening enough to qualify as proof of involvement, but they were certainly incriminating. I prepared myself to simply sit back and continue to listen for other clues throughout what was sure to be a rather nauseating night when the car went over a bump, upsetting one of the precariously stacked boxes.

The contents spilled across the floor at my feet.

Graphite laughed. "Oh, don't mind that stuff. Just throw it back in the box. They're left over from my move. I keep forgetting to bring them inside."

I'd just grabbed a handful of sheet music when I caught sight of something frighteningly familiar. Except when I'd seen it last, it was covered in blood.

The shoe seemed to match the one I'd found in Jason's dumpster. My heart hammered in my chest as I stared at it. I stayed crouched over without moving for so long that Wendy nudged me.

"You okay?" she whispered.

I glanced at Ginger and Graphite. They were too wrapped up in batting their eyes at each other to notice me. I swallowed hard, holding up the shoe.

Wendy shook her head. "What?" she mouthed.

I jabbed my finger at it, widening my eyes in an attempt to make her understand my silent communication.

Wendy stared in incomprehension.

"This is the matching shoe," I whispered.

"*The* shoe?" she hissed. "Like the bloody one?"

I waved my hand to quiet her. I froze when Ginger spoke without taking her eyes from Graphite.

"Have something to share with the class, Frannie?"

"Oh, you know," Wendy said, speaking for my ears alone. "Just finding evidence of a murder."

I shushed her with a finger to my lips and a glare. "I was just telling Wendy that I've never seen so much sheet music in my life. You really are some musician, Graphite."

The flattery was painful, but it did the trick. Soon Graphite was going off about the blood, sweat, and tears that had gone into making his new album, giving me time to collect my thoughts.

There it was: the piece of evidence that just might make the misery I'd subjected Wendy to worthwhile. I was sure that this shoe went with the bloodstained one that had scared me to death the night of the murder.

My heart sank when I remembered that I didn't have the bloodied shoe to show the police. Who would believe me when I told them that I'd found its partner without the incriminating other half of the evidence?

I sent Wendy a silent nod that begged her to trust me as I watched Ginger and Graphite giggle together like school kids.

Surely he'll drop another bit of evidence at some point during the night, and when he does, I'll find a way to use it as evidence that links him to the murder.

Oh my... I'm in the car with a murderer.

"Well, ladies, here we are."

I pulled myself from my investigative musings to glance at the bar he'd chosen. I had to admit that the place had a cool, eclectic look to it, even from the outside.

"It looks so fantastic!" Ginger squealed as she jumped out of the car.

"It's seriously called *The Hang*?" Wendy scoffed, pointing to the sign shining above us.

"Apparently. Graphite sure can pick 'em, huh?"

"I guess so. All I have to say is that I think that since we found that"—she leaned in closer, lowering her voice—"shoe in the car, we should call it a night."

"Leaving now would look suspicious, and you know it. After all, if he *is* a murderer, we don't want to announce it and make him angry. Stick it out for just a little longer, champ. I have a feeling we're going to find a few more clues tonight."

Though she looked doubtful, Wendy followed me into the bar.

It took all of thirty seconds for me to notice that I was woefully underdressed. Though Wendy and I had made fun of Ginger's outfit back at the apartment, I realized now that it suited *The Hang*. Graphite wasn't exactly wearing fancy clothes, but his skinny jeans, collared shirt, and colossal, black earrings worked with the vibe of this place. The countertops were black granite. The booths lining the walls were black as well, causing the crimson-red tablecloths on the tables down the center of the room to pop. It was the same intense red that had stained the snow-white tennis shoe. My faded khakis and T-shirt looked sorely out of place.

"I love this place!" Ginger squealed. The way she hung onto Graphite's arm reminded me of a baby monkey I saw at the zoo once.

"It's the opposite of small-town," Wendy said as Graphite and Ginger walked ahead of us. "I doubt a single one of Golden's citizens has ever set foot in a joint like this." Though I could tell that she was trying to hide it, I caught the fascination in her eyes as she glanced around. "So, what other clues do you expect to get from Pea Gravel tonight?"

"If I knew, we wouldn't have to search them out, would we?" I pulled Wendy to one of the sleek, black booths and yanked her down beside me. Ginger was dragging Graphite toward the stage, where a live band was rocking out. Seems that in spite of the fact we weren't in Kansas anymore, she wanted to try and get up on the stage at all costs. "We just need to sit back and watch out for anything that might prove that he murdered Dale."

Wendy exhaled. "Okay, fine, but you owe me a martini."

"Coming up."

I left the table to get our drinks, figuring buying Wendy's was a small price to pay for an investigating buddy. I'd just ordered when a strange, creeping sensation caused my spine to tingle, as if I were being watched. I turned around but saw only a sea of unfamiliar customers. I glanced back at our table to find Wendy looking with disgust at the front of the stage, where Ginger was dancing with Graphite. Graphite was headbanging while she jumped up and down to the beat of the drums.

I glanced around the bar one more time before turning back to the counter.

Calm down, Frannie. You're just spooked because you found the bloody shoe's other half in the back of the car of a wannabe rock star who is dating your friend. And might be a murderer.

I turned back to get our drinks, but the creepy feeling was back in a moment.

"You're being ridiculous," I muttered to myself as I scooped up our martinis, forcing myself not to glance around like a scared child, though I was tempted.

"I should require you to pay me a steeper price for coming along for this," Wendy said when I set her martini in front of her. "Playing detective is a whole lot harder than I thought."

"It's not all that bad. You just don't like Graphite." Though I'd sworn that my feeling of being watched was silly, I couldn't resist the urge to look around.

"Is something wrong?" Wendy asked.

I shrugged. "No, I don't think so . . ." It was then that I spotted a woman watching me from the booth across the room. She wore a neon-yellow hoodie, and there was no mistaking the fact that her eyes were on me.

Maybe she saw you with Graphite. What if she knows something? She could even be his accomplice.

My throat constricted.

What if Graphite really is the murderer and this is a trap? He might be planning to murder us all the way he did Dale.

I shook my head. I needed to get a hold of myself. There was no way that Ginger could be dating a murderer . . . right? Now that I was face to face with the idea, it felt unfathomable. The bloody shoe in the dumpster and Dale's body in the chest had been planted to incriminate Jason. Perhaps someone had planted the matching shoe to implicate Graphite.

The woman watched me for a moment longer before she quickly slipped out of the booth and scurried around the corner.

"I'm going to go use the restroom, Wendy. I'll be right back."

Wendy grabbed my arm. "You're not thinking of ditching, are you? This was your idea—"

"I'm not ditching you, I'm just using the restroom. Promise." After prying Wendy's hand off of my arm, I power walked in the direction of the woman who'd appeared so interested in me. I glanced around, worried that I'd lost her, when I ran smack-dab into someone as I rounded the last booth before reaching the exit.

"Gosh!" I exclaimed, pulling backward. "I'm so sorry . . ." I trailed off. I recognized the hooded woman. The hoodie looked even more garish up close. I only knew of one person who I'd ever seen wear such an outlandish color.

I took a few steps back, gawking in disbelief. It seemed Wendy had underestimated the daring nature of Golden's citizens. Clearly there *was* one bold enough to venture into a joint that was a step up from the Wine Jug.

I hurried up to her and hissed, "Mrs. Jeffries! "What made you think to visit *The Hang*? It doesn't really seem like your type of place." I noticed the binoculars around her neck before she had a chance to answer. The sight of them left no doubt in my mind; she was following Graphite.

"I believe I might have located a new suspect," Mrs. Jeffries said, pulling off the hood of her sweatshirt to adjust the ruffled shirt collar beneath it. She nodded toward the stage. "Mr. Rock Star over there."

"You're following Graphite? How did you even know about him?"

"I heard Mrs. DeLeon say that the new guy in Ben's band was angry with Dale."

Of course. I was silly to think that Wendy and I were the only ones that Mrs. DeLeon had spilled this juicy detail to.

Mrs. Jeffries looked at the stage, where Graphite was still dancing with Ginger. "He hasn't done anything suspicious yet, but I'm sure he will."

"Maybe." I tried to sound undisturbed but couldn't quite manage it. It seemed the sinking feeling I'd had about Graphite this evening might not be moot.

Darn you, detective instincts. Why does it have to be Ginger's new crush?

"Ginger is pretty taken with him, isn't she?"

I looked back at Mrs. Jeffries to find a knowing expression on her face. I shrugged. "Yeah. I guess rock-n-roll guys are Ginger's type."

Rock-n-roll guys with tempers. Tempers that make them fit to kill?

"I thought you suspected Mrs. DeLeon," I said.

Mrs. Jeffries shook her head. "I was just making an observation when I told you about her, my dear. I didn't really expect you to go running in that direction because of *one* remark."

I chuckled. "Of course not. So, you're pretty sure that Graphite murdered Dale, huh?"

"I'd bet money on it." Mrs. Jeffries wagged her finger at me. "And what about your friend Ginger? I'd be careful around her if I were you."

I laughed. "I don't think that her poor taste in men is any reason for me to be 'careful' around her."

Mrs. Jeffries gripped my arm. "It is if she helped her new boyfriend get his way. Dale was the only one standing between Graphite and his debut here in Golden, right? His debut at the Living History Day Festival?"

I shook my head. "Ginger would never involve herself with something like that, trust me."

Mrs. Jeffries shrugged. "I hope you're right. But a true detective never counts out a potential suspect." She squared her shoulders, her chin lifting like a soldier. "It's important that all investigators remain unbiased. It's the only way to get justice."

I tried to summon a response but came up empty. There was no way Ginger was involved. No way . . .

Mrs. Jeffries pressed the binoculars to her eyes. "His type can't be trusted," she said.

"If by 'his type' you mean guys who have gauge earrings, I think—"

"No, no. I mean young men like that who get up on stage with all of those speakers blaring around them. Youngsters these days think that nothing will make them go deaf."

I groaned when I turned to find that Graphite and Ginger had finally managed to get a spot on the stage. Wendy was looking just as miserable as last time as she watched them dance amongst the musicians.

Mrs. Jeffries motioned toward me with the binoculars. "I'm going to get out of here before he sees me. But remember what I said, Frannie: keep an eye on Ginger there."

I watched Mrs. Jeffries exit the building, wishing that her words didn't bother me. But they did, not because I suspected my friend in anyway, but because now I'd never stop worrying for her safety.

CHAPTER TWELVE

I sat in the diner down the street from *The Nugget.* I took another long drink of my chocolate malt before looking at my watch. Wendy was late.

I tapped my fingers on the table, exhaling. Sure enough, after talking with Mrs. Jeffries at *The Hang,* I'd felt sick over her words and had a fitful night. I knew that I had to tell Wendy. I would explode if I didn't

If she'd only get here . . .

As if on cue, the glass doors of the diner swung open as Wendy came tumbling through. She raced over to my table as quickly as her stilettos would allow. "Sorry I'm late."

"You should be," I snapped more sharply than I intended. "I have some big news, and you've made me suffer waiting for you."

Wendy motioned to my nearly empty malt glass. "Doesn't look like you've been suffering too terribly. I think I'll take one of those too."

I forced myself to wait as Wendy flagged down a waitress and ordered a chocolate malt and French fries.

"Okay, so what's this big news?" she asked, settling back against the plastic cover of the checkered booth.

I took a deep breath before answering in a low voice. "I saw something last night at *The Hang.*"

Wendy rolled her eyes. "So did I and I never want to see it again."

"I'm not talking about Ginger and Graphite dancing on the stage. Would you listen to me, Wendy?"

Wendy held up her hands in surrender. "Okay, relax. What did you see? A hot guy? A cool outfit?"

"No. I saw Mrs. Jeffries."

Wendy blinked at me in confusion. "Wait, what? When?"

"Do you remember when I went to the restroom just after getting our drinks?"

Wendy nodded.

"I wasn't using the restroom," I said. "I was following someone in a neon-yellow hoodie I'd spotted across the room."

Wendy laughed. "Mrs. Jeffries would forget to ditch the neon colors even when she's trying to be incognito."

"You're still not listening to me, Wendy. I have to tell you what she was doing there."

Wendy shrugged. "So, tell me."

I rested my elbows on the table, lowering my voice even further. "She was spying on Graphite."

"What's the big deal? That's why we were there too, isn't it?" Wendy became fully absorbed in her milkshake as the waiter plunked a large order of fries and a bottle of ketchup on the corner of the table.

Usually the thick-cut house fries would make my mouth water, but right now my stomach felt sour due to my disturbing thoughts about Ginger. Or maybe I'd just gulped down my malt too fast. Either way, the fries held no appeal. "Yes, we were there to spy on Graphite. But Mrs. Jeffries brought up something I hadn't even thought about: if Graphite was involved in Dale's murder, that might mean Ginger is in terrible danger."

Wendy set down her milkshake, coughing. It was a moment before she composed herself enough to speak. "You can't be serious. Besides, you know Mrs. Jeffries. She's always saying whatever comes into her head."

"That's what I thought at first too," I said. "But what about the tennis shoe in the back of his car?"

Wendy waved a French fry at me before dunking it into the pool of ketchup she'd squirted onto a napkin. It was so red. Why was everything red like the blood on that darn shoe?

"There's no guarantee that the sneaker you saw in Graphite's car was the one that went with the dumpster shoe. You know that I'm not a fan of Pea Gravel. But he might not be the murderer, so I don't think there's any reason to worry about Ginger."

I crossed my arms, surveying her with open skepticism. "Well, it seems to me that when it comes to evidence, most of it is stacked up against him."

"Mm-hmm, I'm not so sure," Wendy said around her straw as she took another drink of her malt.

"We can't be sure of anything right now," I insisted. "But I think that finding a shoe that closely resembles the one I found in the dumpster *in* one of our suspect's cars isn't something that should be ignored. Don't you think that you should at least mention it to Brenda?"

Wendy waved off the suggestion immediately. "She'd say that the evidence is too flimsy. I can just hear her laughing at us now."

I slumped back against the booth, crossing my arms. "I can't believe you're being so prim about talking to her. She's your *sister,* for Pete's Sake!"

Wendy shook her head. "It's like I said, I just think that accusing Graphite of murder because he has a similar-looking shoe is a leap. Besides, I think that you'll rethink your conclusions when you hear what I have to tell you."

I frowned. "Okay . . ."

Wendy leaned in. "I heard that Baker Pierre made another mysterious trip to the dumpster at Jason's apartment again last night."

"From who?"

"Mrs. Jeffries."

I threw my hands over my face. "Man! That woman sure gets around. First it's Pierre she's trying to implicate, then it's Mrs. DeLeon, then it's Graphite, then it's Ginger . . . Now it's Pierre *again?*"

"She's being nosy about this whole thing—there's no doubt," Wendy admitted. "But I think she has a good point about Baker

Pierre. If you ask me, his behavior has been the sketchiest of all of late. And then there was all that stuff he was doing on the phone."

"What stuff?" I jolted when Wendy pounded the metal milkshake refill container that sat beside her malt glass down on the table.

"Remember how he was pounding things around while you two were on the phone? If you ask me, he's got motive and enough suspicious activity to make him a *real* suspect."

I nodded slowly, pondering her words. "I kept thinking that it would be a good idea to have a word with Baker Pierre. I guess now is the time, huh?"

"Yep," Wendy agreed. "Plus, it'll help you to stop thinking about Graphite. Honestly, I don't think that guy is smart enough to orchestrate a murder all on his own, no matter how angry he was about the cancellation of Living History Day. But Baker Pierre might."

I still didn't like the idea of implicating someone I knew as well as Baker Pierre. But I had to admit that it would be a relief to divert the accusations as far away from Ginger as possible.

It was time to visit the bakery.

CHAPTER THIRTEEN

*W*endy and I were immediately enveloped by the mouth-watering aromas of fresh-baked breads and sugary-sweet confections upon stepping into Baker Pierre's shop. Today the diner's house fries hadn't succeeded in giving me an appetite, but the sight and smell of the gooey cinnamon rolls behind the glass display case sure did.

Pierre popped up from behind the counter at the summoning of the bell over the door. His smile stretched from ear to ear as he stood, abandoning the pastry wrap and paper bags he'd been sorting.

"Mademoiselles! Welcome! What can I do for you today?"

"Hi, Baker Pierre," I greeted. I took a moment to sniff the air exaggeratedly. "It smells heavenly in here."

"Ah, you must be smelling the lavender mint muffins that I just pulled out of the oven!"

"Lavender mint?" Wendy repeated uncertainly.

"It's a new recipe. Very innovative. I'll let you two lovely mademoiselles sample them free of charge."

He disappeared into the kitchen before we could respond.

"Acacia bundt cake?" Wendy read, leaning toward the glass case. "Looks like Pierre's getting pretty creative."

"Did I hear bundt cake?" Pierre called as he breezed back into the room holding two muffins.

"Wendy was just saying that your Acacia bundt cake sounds very . . . interesting," I said.

Baker Pierre handed Wendy and me each a muffin. "One of many new recipes." A forlorn expression passed over his face as he scanned the rows of baked goods in the display. "I'm afraid desperate situations call for desperate measures. I need to think up a new best seller in order to make up for the revenue I'll lose without the Living History Day sales."

"Oh, that's right." I did my best not to appear suspicious as I studied the free sample in my hand. I was relieved to find that the muffin didn't look half as strange as it sounded. Still, I was leery of the combination, so when I took a bite, it was with the utmost caution. Once I had, I looked to Wendy, who had also bitten into her sample. We shared a look of surprise.

"Wow, I'm . . . impressed," Wendy said.

"Do you think it could be my next best seller?" Pierre asked, clasping his hands hopefully in front of him like an eager child.

"I don't know about best seller," I chimed in. "But it's definitely a surprise. It sounds like such an odd combination. But it's actually alright."

Pierre snapped his fingers. "Just alright isn't going to be good enough. I need to find something that is off the charts good, sensational."

"Haven't cinnamon rolls always been a big seller for you?" Wendy pointed out.

Pierre conceded with a nod. "They have, but I would have to sell triple the number of cinnamon rolls I usually do in order to make up for the proceeds I'll lose from Living History Day."

Wendy and I exchanged a glance.

"I'm sure you will," I said. "What other pastries have you tried?"

Pierre's gaze rolled to the ceiling as he counted on his fingers. "Apple dumpling scones, marzipan sweet rolls, Froot Loop macaroons, marmalade pie . . . I've tried everything."

"You sure have when you start employing breakfast cereal in your baking," Wendy remarked with a chuckle.

"And how have they worked out?" I probed. "I would think that the bakery would be overflowing with baked goods by now. Where are you hiding all these delectable confections?"

Pierre raised his hands in resignation. "Alas, most of them did not meet Baker Pierre's high standards and therefore will never be available for purchase."

"You mean you threw them all away?" I clarified.

"So it's the dumpster that is overflowing rather than the pastry cases," Wendy said. She laughed, shaking her head. "Murphy, the garbage man, is sure going to be surprised when he empties your trash. Wouldn't be surprised if he had to make an extra trip. Murphy has been known to charge extra for a bigger garbage output than usual, you know."

Pierre's brows wiggled conspiratorially. "Ah, but I have already figured out how to avoid this, *mon cheri.*" Pierre tapped the side of his head with one finger. "You underestimate the intelligence of the French."

I frowned in confusion. "What do you mean?"

Pierre leaned closer, motioning for Wendy and me to do the same. He lowered his voice, though we were the only occupants of the bakery. "Murphy can't double charge me if he doesn't know he's collecting my trash."

My mouth opened in surprise as understanding dawned. "You mean you dumped your trash elsewhere?"

Pierre crossed his arms over his chest with a nod, looking endlessly pleased with his own slyness. "I'm entrusting you girls with my secret because I know you can both be trusted. But I'm not telling anyone where I dumped the trash." He made a show of zipping his lips and locking an imaginary lock before tossing the imaginary key over his shoulder. "I'll never tell."

Hate to break it to you, but your secret isn't quite as secret as you thought. Sorry, monsieur.

"First Acaia bundt cake and now this act of sneakiness from you,"

Wendy said with an exaggerated shake of her head. "Will wonders ever cease?"

Pierre laughed. "The French. I tell you, we have much to offer."

"I believe you." Though it was far from the best muffin I'd ever had, I took another bite of my free sample. The fact that Pierre had only been dumping failed baking attempts and not the evidence of Dale's murder into Jason's dumpster made me want to give the lavender mint muffin a fair chance. Strangely enough, the more I ate, the more the odd combination grew on me.

Pierre might be onto something so long as he can convince his customers to bear with the strangeness of his new pastries to get past the first bite.

"I'm sure you'll come up with something great during the course of your experimentation," I said. "You'll show this whole town why you're positively irreplaceable, no matter what other bakers exist outside of Golden."

Pierre cleared his throat. "The one I really wish could be witness to my success in rising from the ashes is that Dale Meyers. But he got what was coming to him." The baker shrugged as he grabbed a skillet from behind the counter. I wondered what it was doing there, but what concerned me more was the possibility that he might reenact his desire to hit Dearly Departed Dale over the head with his weapon of choice. I was relieved when he simply held the skillet in his hands, looking down at it thoughtfully. "*C'est la vie.*"

"Yeah, *c'est la vie,*" Wendy echoed, tossing me a meaningful glance as she took another bite of her muffin. Clearly she'd gotten past the initial suspiciousness of the pastry as well.

"We persist until we succeed, no?" Pierre set aside the skillet, reaching below the counter once again, this time in order to produce two paper pastry bags. "You ladies have been so helpful in providing feedback on my lavender mint muffins. Would you care to take a piece of acai cake with you as well?"

Wendy shrugged, obviously feeling more adventurous after trying Pierre's newest muffin. "Sure, why not?"

I agreed to take a slice as well, but my thoughts weren't on innovative baked goods.

Baker Pierre was right: one had to persist until one succeeded. The investigation was not over. But Wendy and I had our work cut out for us now. Relieved as I was to cross Pierre off of our list, there was no avoiding the fact that doing so implicated someone who was dearly beloved by Ginger: Graphite.

CHAPTER FOURTEEN

*A*s I lay in bed wrapped in a blanket, having donned my favorite flannel pajamas, I couldn't quite bring myself to focus on the book in my hands. I always loved getting in a chapter or two of a good book before bedtime, but tonight the mystery story before me held little interest. It was hard to be enthralled by a fake crime when a real, live one was running rampant through my hometown.

I finally gave up, pressing a bookmark between the pages and tossing the paperback onto the bedside table. I picked up the handwritten suspect list that Wendy and I had compiled, running my eyes over it for the thousandth time. Ms. DeLeon and Mrs. Jeffries names were still on the list, though I had a feeling I would soon be crossing them out.

Mrs. Jeffries was likely only involved in the case because she found chasing a murderer thrilling. I found it highly improbable that she would have followed us all the way to *The Hang* if she were the murderer. Between that and the peeking into windows looking for clues, I firmly believed that the only thing she was guilty of was excessive nosiness.

As for Ms. DeLeon, she was sore about being knocked off of the decorating committee, no doubt about it. However, it appeared she'd been implicated by Mrs. Jeffries in her zeal to believe that anyone in Golden could be the criminal we sought. Besides, those two were always at war with each other for one reason or another. I personally did not think it likely that she would have the audacity to kill off Dale and frame Jason for it.

Wendy and I had unanimously agreed to clear Baker Pierre of all suspicion. His biggest struggle lately had been coming up with a new and innovative pastry selection, giving him little time to plot a murder.

Graphite's place on the list had been significantly solidified by me when I found the shoe I believed to match the bloodstained one from the dumpster in his car. Wendy was skeptical and still thought that I might be jumping to conclusions. But as far as I was concerned, no one knew what Graphite was capable of. He might not seem particularly clever, as Wendy had pointed out, but I wouldn't be ready to cross him off until I believed him innocent beyond a reasonable doubt.

Then there was Jason, the suspect who'd ignited this whole investigation.

I knew that I should go and see Jason, but I couldn't quite bring myself to visit the jail again. I wanted to go when I had solid evidence against someone—evidence that proved which Golden citizen had killed Dale.

True, our suspect list was shrinking. Still, I would need to get a few things straight before I could be sure of who was really guilty of murder. The trouble was that I didn't know how to get the reassurance I needed to make a conviction.

I was deep into mulling this over when my cell phone rang. I frowned down at the caller ID. It was Ben.

Though I was tempted to decline the call, I thought better of it when I remembered that anyone could present valuable evidence that would help me with the case at any time. I'd best answer.

"Hello?"

"Hey. How's your evening, Frannie?"

I cringed. He sounded just as nervous over the phone as he did in person. I could just see him fidgeting as he talked to me, switching the phone back and forth from one ear to the other.

"It's fine. How's yours?"

"Just fine."

An awkward silence ensued.

"Uh . . . is there something you called for?"

"Oh, yeah." Ben sounded as if he'd just remembered that it had been him who'd initiated the phone call. "I wanted to ask you a question . . . and I'm hoping you'll say yes."

My heart dropped.

Oh no, please don't invite me to go on a double date with you, Ginger, and Graphite. I'll go pretty far for the sake of investigating, but that is too far, buddy.

"Would you like to go out with me?"

I covered the phone so he wouldn't hear me sigh. "I know that Ginger is hanging out with Graphite and they thought that hanging out as a group would be cool and all, but I just don't think—"

"No."

I blinked in shock. This was the first time Ben had had the gumption to cut me off when I was talking. Ever.

"I mean, uh," he stammered. "I wasn't trying to plan a double date. I was thinking it would be just me and you."

My entire body went cold. "What?" My mind whirled. My almost-fiancé was in jail, for heaven's sake. What sort of guy had the gall to ask out a girl in my situation? I rolled my eyes, reminding myself that it wasn't every day that a girl found herself in my situation.

Lucky me.

"To be honest, Frannie," Ben continued, uncertainly. "I've been wanting to ask you out for a long time. I just wasn't sure if you would say yes."

"And you think I would now because . . ." The last thing I wanted to be was mean. Though conversations with Ben were always awkward, I had nothing against the guy. But I was having a hard time believing what I was hearing. The suggestion of me hanging out with Ben was reasonable coming from Graphite or even Ginger, since she was head over heels for Graphite. But I couldn't believe Ben would be bold enough to ask me out on a date while my boyfriend was behind bars.

"I just . . . hoped since Jason . . .well, you know . . ."

"Since he might be convicted of a murder he didn't commit, I would be ready to go out with someone else?" A hysterical note had made its way into my voice. I took a deep breath in an attempt to get a hold of myself. Surely Ben was just being oblivious. He'd finally gathered up the courage to ask me out, but the timing was all wrong.

Yes, that's all it is. Don't overreact about this, Frannie.

"Thanks for the offer, but I don't think so, Ben."

Another awkward silence ensued, but this time, instead of simply being an annoyance, it was appreciated because it gave me a moment to think. If Mrs. Jeffries had told me to keep an eye on Ginger of how close she was to Graphite, wouldn't it make sense to watch out for Ben too?

He was, after all, the person Graphite knew best in Golden besides Ginger.

"I guess that's it then," Ben finally said. I could imagine his face—like that of a sad puppy.

"Well, uh, where were you thinking of taking me?" I asked. There was no way I wanted to go on a date with Ben, but I hoped that at least being kind about his attempts was called for, awkward though it may be. Plus, if I kept him talking, maybe I could make sure he wasn't in any immediate danger from Graphite and bonus if I got any information that actually helped me with the case.

"The diner, maybe?"

Romantic.

"Oh. Why there?"

"It's where Graphite takes Ginger sometimes. We've gone there a lot since they started going out."

The murder had only taken place a couple of days earlier. That meant that if they'd been there a couple of times, one of those times could have been on the night of Dale's murder, giving them an alibi. And if they weren't there . . .

"When was the last time you went?"

The night of Dale's murder, perhaps?

For the first time I was grateful that Ben was cuckoo about me as it made him unaware of the rather blatant connections I was making.

Ben cleared his throat.

My heart pounded in my chest. This could clear Graphite of all suspicion. If he'd been at the diner on Saturday night, then he couldn't have been sneaking Dale's limp body into Jason's apartment, could he?

And yet, if you clear Graphite, who does that leave on the suspect list?

Jason.

I took a deep breath in a failed attempt to calm the mad fluttering of my heart.

Don't freak out yet. The investigation isn't over.

"Were you at the diner with Graphite on Saturday night?" I asked.

"Saturday?" Ben asked, with a warble in his voice. "Uh no, I don't think we were there Saturday."

"Hmm. Alright, Ben, sorry but I've got to run," I said, pleased with how nonchalant my voice sounded.

"Yeah, okay me too," Ben said, clearing his throat. "Well, anyway, I said what I called for so . . . I guess I'll be seeing you."

"Yep, see you."

I hung up the phone, staring down at the dark screen, thinking. At any other time, I would have simply been appalled that Ben had asked me out. Now, I saw our conversation as another lead, a way to find out what Graphite had been up to the night of the murder.

Believing the worst of my friends and neighbors was getting easier and easier. I wasn't sure if that was a good thing, but it did help me feel as if I was getting somewhere with the investigation.

My hope was that I would be able to clear Jason's name. I had to check out the biggest suspect on my list, and at the moment, that happened to be Graphite.

I knew where to make my next investigative stop: the diner.

CHAPTER FIFTEEN

Upon entering the diner, I wasn't sure exactly what I was looking for. What I did know was that Golden was a small town by every definition, and everyone recognized newcomers. Someone would remember Graphite.

"Eating alone?"

I smiled at the brunette waitress, Margie, who was wearing a checkered apron.

"Yes, it's just me."

I was led to a corner booth where a glossy brochure-style menu prominently displayed the milkshake of the month to be chocolate s'mores. The decadent picture made my mouth water.

"What can I start you out with?" Margie asked.

"I think I'll get one of your milkshakes of the month."

"Excellent choice." Margie was about to turn away when I stopped her.

"Do you think I could ask you something?"

Margie flicked the pencil in her hand toward me. "Shoot."

I leaned forward, lowering my voice. "Have you happened to notice Ginger and Ben come in a lot lately with a guy who is new in town? He has—"

"A rocker-type look," Margie finished. "Yeah, I saw them in here on last Thursday. They sat in that booth over there by the window." She chuckled. "Ginger was all over him."

"No surprise there," I responded dryly. "How late did they stay? Do you remember?" My mind was racing.

Thursday . . . That was two days before Dale's murder.

Margie frowned in thought. "Almost until the end of my shift. I would say they left at about five thirty."

My heart pounded in my chest.

"Did you notice anything . . . suspicious going on? I mean, did you hear what they were talking about or anything like that?"

Margie shook her head vigorously. "Oh, no! I never listen in on the conversations of my customers!"

I raised my hands. "Of course you don't, Margie. I didn't mean to insinuate that. I was just hoping to get an idea of what sort of vibe their conversation had."

Margie glanced around again. She tucked the pencil behind her ear before turning back to me. "Well, I did notice something. I don't know if it's important or not. Could be nothing."

"Tell me," I whispered.

Margie threw another furtive glance around the diner before continuing. "They were all sitting together just talking and laughing. They were really loud, actually. I think the entire restaurant could hear them. The rocker boy kept telling Ginger what a rock star she is."

I rolled my eyes but couldn't help smiling. "Sounds about right."

"Then Ginger got up to use the ladies room, leaving the two gentlemen alone."

"Go on."

"Ben and the rocker boy waited until Ginger was gone before they leaned really close together and started talking all secretive-like."

My heart raced and I took a deep breath to keep from launching myself out of the booth.. "You couldn't hear what they said?" I raised my hand. "I know you don't listen in on customers' conversations. But maybe you heard something by accident?"

Margie lowered her voice, "I did hear one thing. Ben said something like 'But we really have to keep it quiet, man. Are you sure no one will know? I've been wanting to date Frannie for a long time, but do you really think this is the best way? And don't you think Ginger will be upset?'"

Margie gave me a pointed look.

My heart jumped into my throat. "Are you sure that's what he said? I mean *really* sure? He said my name?"

Margie nodded. "You know Ben's been after you a long time. Shoot, Frannie, the whole town knows."

I swallowed my dread.

This is all my fault.

Margie leaned in closer. "And then the rocker boy was like 'Trust me, dude, this is the way to go. It's killing two birds with one stone, no pun intended. You don't want to let Dale Meyers run all over you, do you?' At least that's what I think he said," she rushed on. "Like I told you, I don't listen to customers' conversations."

"I understand," I said, my heart continuing to pound. "But I get the gist." I forced a smile, having no desire to let Margie in on how much her words freaked me out. "Thanks for telling me. You've been a great help."

I leaned back in my chair as Margie scurried off to make the milkshake I no longer had any interest in, my mind moving at one hundred miles per hour.

Margie had said that Ben and Graphite only started acting suspicious once Ginger was out of earshot. Ben was also worried that whatever they were talking about would upset Ginger.

I needed to unravel the meaning behind Graphite and Ben's enigmatic words. Graphite appeared to be the instigator here considering what he'd said about getting back at Dale Meyers. But Ben's comment about just wanting to go on a date was equally disturbing.

He'd just asked me out.

I thought back on the way he'd hung around the jail . . . even pestered Brenda about how long they would search for the criminal before prosecuting Jason.

Was it possible that Ben had helped frame Jason so he'd have a clear pathway to me?

I shook my head, staring at the milkshake Margie had just delivered. I'd never thought of myself as any sort of a catch. I was, after all, once divorced and not exactly the type men fell to their knees before. But Ben had been after me for a long time. Perhaps he just needed a push from a gutsier friend?

And let the record show: both Ben and Graphite had good reason to be angry with Dale. Oh no, I wasn't ready for this . . .

I grabbed a huge chunk of chocolate-covered graham cracker off the top of my milkshake, popping it into my mouth as I continued to think. Whether she was willing to admit it or not, Margie had been a witness to this condemning conversation, so that was in our favor. Still, I would need more evidence if I wanted to present an airtight case.

I toyed with the handle of the milkshake spoon on the table, far from pleased with the next step I'd have to take. I needed to talk straight with Ginger. It seemed pretty obvious that if Graphite and Ben had hatched (and carried out!) this heinous plan, she needed to be warned.

But I would need to be careful. She was dead gone on Graphite, and I would need to tread lightly if I wanted to gain her cooperation.

I was going to need Wendy for this one. I flagged Margie, wasting no time in asking for a to-go cup. I would have to drink my milkshake on the run. The tasks I had before me couldn't wait.

I stood outside the diner, to-go cup of milkshake in my hand as I dialed Wendy. When she didn't pick up, I tried again.

You know that we have an investigation to complete, Wendy. For heaven's sake, pick up!

Wendy answered on the fourth ring, her tone inescapably miffed. "Frannie, I hope whatever you're calling about is *blessed* important. You know that calling over and over again when someone doesn't answer is a show of bad manners, right?"

"I hope I didn't interrupt anything," I said, though I knew the apology was unconvincing. "It's just that I've made a pretty big discovery on the case."

"Great," Wendy responded dismissively.

I frowned. "That's all you have to say? I need to tell you about it."

"There will be plenty of time to chase after another lead tomorrow. At the moment, I'm still recovering from the aftereffects of *The*

Hang." She laughed without humor. "I've figured it out. They don't call it *The Hang* because it's a place to 'hang' out. They call it that because it gives you a *hangover*, even if you don't drink. And just being there makes you want to *hang* yourself."

I shook my head in bewilderment. "Wendy, I don't understand what's going on with you. You seemed just fine when we were at the bakery. What happened? I feel like you've flipped on me—like you don't care about the case at all."

Wendy exhaled. I could just imagine her shifting her weight on her alligator heels, her eyes rolling heavenward. "Okay, you want to know the truth? Your brother and I got in a fight today about how much time I've been spending tromping around with you."

I laughed. "You can't be serious."

"Oh, I'm dead serious. He says that I've been spending too much time 'playing detective' as he calls it, and he wants me to take a day off. I get it. I have been AWOL every single day and night since Jason got himself into this fix. I don't know if you've noticed, but your brother isn't exactly thrilled about the fact that you're defending a potential murderer. Not exactly the brother-in-law he had in mind."

"Jason didn't get himself into anything!" I cried. "He was set up! I can't believe we're even having this conversation! And I have a good mind to call my brother and give him a piece of my mind. This is important!"

"Listen, rushing out to continue investigating tonight isn't going to change anything. It can wait until tomorrow. I have a thoroughly peeved husband to deal with. If I've got his annoyance under control by tomorrow, I'll call you. Bye."

"Wendy, wait!" I stared out at the diner parking lot in stunned silence as she hung up on me. I shoved my cell into my purse, taking a drink from the extra-long, plastic straw Margie had put in my milkshake to replace the dine-in metal one, thinking hard. I knew that I needed to talk to Ginger, there was no getting around that. Investigating was positively addictive, and I wanted nothing more than to charge forward with my plans with or without Wendy.

"Darn you, Wendy," I muttered as I made my way to my car. I liked to think of myself as strong and independent (I'd survived starting over after getting divorced before the age of twenty-five, after all!). But I was smart enough to know that facing Ginger with the news that her dearly beloved Graphite had a hand in setting Jason up as a murderer wasn't a good idea. I could just see Ginger having a full-on meltdown. I needed backup to weather that kind of drama unless I wanted to risk ruining our friendship beyond repair.

Turning my car toward home took all of the self-control that I could muster. By the time I'd parked in the lot in front of my apartment building, I'd come up with a plan. I was going to chase this lead tonight. But not without Wendy.

All I had to do was head to her and my brother's house that evening. By then, they'd have had a chance to kiss and make up over Wendy's absence since Jason's arrest. I would get Wendy to come with me to speak with Ginger if it was the last thing I did. I felt confident that I could pull this off considering the slyness I'd employed thus far in the investigation. I was getting better and better at being sneaky with each passing day. Besides, even if my brother didn't want Wendy to go, he was an early-to-bed type of person. My brother had always been a spoilsport when it came to staying up late and kept "grandpa hours" as I'd called them as a kid. I'd heard Wendy complain more than once about the fact that they never got to finish movies together because he was always snoring by eight thirty p.m. This would make sneaking Wendy out of the house a whole lot easier if that's what it took. All I had to do was make Wendy see the importance of chasing this lead tonight. She'd be out of the house and back in before my brother even knew she was gone.

From there, we'd confront Ginger. Together, I was sure that we'd be able to make her see reason and save her from her deadly attraction to Graphite before it was too late.

CHAPTER SIXTEEN

*I*t was dark when I set out for Wendy's house, but I walked down the streets of Golden with confidence. I'd lived here my entire life, and I wasn't going to let one of my hometown's upstanding citizen's reputations be muddied. In reality, Jason was an outsider, but I decided that this was beside the point. I was bound and determined to clear his good name.

I'd opted to leave my car behind, deciding that bringing it along would attract too much attention. True, my brother slept like the dead, but I wasn't going to take any chances.

I power walked down the lamp-lit streets of Golden, intent on making it to my destination. However, an unusual sight near the jail stopped me in my tracks.

I narrowed my gaze. There was a man knocking on the front door. My eyes widened when I realized who it was: Ben.

Without a second thought, I leapt into the bushes just off the sidewalk, crouching low as I watched his every move. Due to the low crime rate in Golden, the jail held the same hours as most of the businesses in town, opening at nine a.m. and closing at five p.m.

Regardless of the sign clearly posted on the door stating that the jail was closed to visitors, Ben was obviously bound and determined to enter. He knocked on the door, glancing furtively around, then trying again when there was no answer. A few moments later, the door opened. It was Brenda.

"What's going on Ben? Is something wrong?" the police officer asked, her brow knit with confusion.

"Yes." Ben's voice was noticeably agitated and his hands fluttered restlessly the same way they did when he couldn't seem to get a grip around me. "I need to ask you something. Can I come in?"

Brenda stepped aside to admit the band leader, leaving me alone in the dark once again. I plopped down in the bushes to wait. Demanding entrance to the police station after hours was far from "normal" activity, and the fact that my newest suspect was doing just that made this an impossible lead not to follow. It seemed Wendy had been wrong: the continuation of this investigation definitely could not wait until tomorrow.

A few minutes later, Ben exited the police station, moving stealthily back down the road toward the Wine Jug, the only establishment in town regularly open after five. I waited until Ben had vanished before venturing out of the bushes and making my way toward the police station. Brenda had already been disturbed once tonight. Now it was my turn.

I rapped on the door. Though I was no criminal like Ben, I couldn't help glancing around me as I waited.

Brenda's face revealed her annoyance the moment she opened the door. "Seriously, does anyone want me to get out of here in time to eat dinner before ten p.m.?"

It seemed today was my day for being a nuisance, but I wasn't going to let that get in the way. "Brenda! I need to talk to you right away."

Brenda exhaled, massaging her temples with her fingers. "You too?"

"Yes. It's about Ben."

Brenda lowered her hands, frowning in confusion. "Ben? Did you just . . .?"

"I was hiding in the bushes."

Brenda scowled at me, glancing down the dark street. "Oh, what the heck. Just come in, Frannie."

I stepped into the dim police station. The only light in the place emanated from the tabletop lamp at Brenda's workstation. Her desk was littered with papers, making me feel slightly guilty that I'd interrupted her. But only slightly. What I had to say was important, and I knew it. I thought about creeping around the corner to say hello to Jason, but immediately thought better of it. Seeing Jason behind bars again would distract me, and I needed to have a clear mind. I would stick to my original plan; I would come for him when I had some good news to share. And right now, I was breathtakingly close to obtaining it.

"Do you want to start by telling me what you were doing hiding in the bushes?" Brenda demanded, leaning against her desk, arms crossed. Directly after the words left her mouth, understanding dawned on the police officer's face. "No way. Are you actually investigating the murder?"

I shrugged helplessly in response.

Brenda threw her head back. "You've got to be kidding me. You were spying on the police station. Really?"

"Not exactly," I objected. "I was just passing by when I noticed Ben. But before you judge me and tell me that I shouldn't be interfering with police business and even though Golden might be small, the police department is as professional as any other city's, hear me out."

Brenda dropped her face into her hands. "Frannie, you've always been an upstanding citizen. You should know better than to go around stirring up trouble, even if the accused is your intended."

My mouth popped open in disbelief. "Stirring up trouble? Me? I'm not the one who killed off Dale Meyers and planted his dead body in someone's apartment. I'm trying to *catch* the crook who is stirring up trouble!"

Brenda exhaled as she glanced at her watch. "Okay, you have two minutes to tell me why you're here. Go."

"Brenda, why was Ben here?" I asked. "What did he want?"

Brenda frowned. "He wanted to know how long we would continue investigating this case before Jason was convicted."

My heart dropped to the pit of my stomach. "He did?"

Brenda leveled a gaze at me. "Is that really so surprising? I'm pretty sure everyone in Golden is asking themselves the same question. Everyone's on the edge of their seats waiting to find out the verdict of who murdered Dale."

I took a deep breath, working hard to calm the pounding of my heart. "It is after learning what I just did."

Brenda's expression screamed skepticism. "And what did you just learn?"

I leaned in closer. "Okay, so get this. I got a tip that Ginger, Graphite, and Ben have been going to the diner a lot So, I went in and talked to Margie, who was working there Thursday night when they were eating, and guess what she told me."

Brenda shrugged. "I don't know. What did she tell you?"

"She told me that when Ginger went to visit the ladies' room, Graphite and Ben started whispering super secretively. She said that Ben was asking Graphite if the plan would work. The plan to *kill* Dale."

I had Brenda's attention now. She stared at me. "Are you sure?"

I nodded. "And then Ben was like 'I don't want to make anyone upset. All I want is to go on a date with her.'"

The confusion had returned to Brenda's face. "That doesn't tell you anything. He could have been talking about anyone."

I shook my head vigorously. "Margie said he mentioned me by name. Plus, the fact that he just called to ask me out on a date."

Brenda laughed. "Are you serious? He's had a crush on you for years. Do you mean to tell me that he's never asked you on a date until now?"

I shook my head. "Never. Acted super awkward and tried to flirt plenty of times. But he's never come out and asked me."

Brenda stared in astonishment. "Maybe that was because you've always had someone, either a husband or a boyfriend. Are you thinking that he's asking you now because—"

"Because Jason is in jail," I hissed beneath my breath. "And he helped put him there! See, Graphite orchestrated the whole thing. He figured that he could get back at Dale Meyers for knocking Ben's band off the program for Living History Day *and* they could frame Jason as the murderer. Win, win."

Brenda's gaze narrowed in thought. "That does change things."

"You're darn right, it does!"

"Alright, I have to admit that you've done some good investigating," Brenda said. "But it still isn't enough to convict anyone. Right now, it's all hearsay."

I lifted my chin, my confidence rising. "Soon we will have all the evidence we need, trust me." I turned on my heels, stalking out of the police station before Brenda had a chance to protest. Wendy and I were on the verge of closing this case, and nothing, not even the technicalities of Golden's police department, was going to stop me.

CHAPTER SEVENTEEN

$\mathscr{T}$he following morning, I received a blank stare of disbelief
from Wendy after I relayed Margie's words about Graphite,
Ben, and Ginger's visit to the diner.

"It can't be," Wendy said, leaning heavily against *The Nugget*'s front
counter. "Do you really think this proves that Graphite . . . and maybe
even Ben are guilty of *murder?*"

"I'm as shocked as you are, Wendy," I said. "But I don't really see
how their words could be misconstrued. They were clearly up to
something, and Ben *did* just ask me out on a date. And both Ben and
Graphite had a lot to lose by being kicked out of the Living History
Day celebration." I shivered. "I don't want to think that someone
we've both known forever helped to set up my boyfriend, but it
appears that way. Unless you think there's something I've missed?"

Wendy's lips scrunched together as she studied the countertop.
"Dang, I can't think of anything. I just can't believe it."

"Me neither."

Wendy crossed her arms over her chest. "So, what do we do now?"

"I've already asked Ginger to meet us here." I exhaled. "I know it'll
be awkward, but someone has to tell her. I'm sure it'll be hard for her
to admit that her rock star crush is up to no good, but she might not
have a choice."

Wendy reached out, gripping my arm reassuringly. "She'll do the right thing. Love is blind, and she is head over heels for Graphite. But she is loyal to you and Jason, so I have confidence in her."

I was about to respond when the bell over the front door jangled, admitting Ginger. I exchanged a glance with Wendy upon noting the band T-shirt she wore. The fact that I'd never seen her wear anything like it, and the fact that it was clearly a couple of sizes too big, left no doubt in my mind that it belonged to Graphite.

Oh dear, this might not be as easy as you were hoping.

"Hey, girls," Ginger greeted, smiling cheekily. "What's cracking?"

"I don't even know how to respond to that question," Wendy chuckled dryly.

"How have you been, Ginger?" I asked, ignoring Wendy completely.

Ginger looked dreamily up to the ceiling. "Oh, you know, just the usual."

"Hanging out with Graphite?" Wendy supplied.

Ginger nodded. She raised her wrist, wagging the bracelet clasped there in our faces. "He's so thoughtful. Look what he gave me."

Wendy rolled her eyes, dismissing the wristlet immediately. However, the sight of it caused my mouth to go dry.

"Wait, let me look at that closer," I said, grabbing Ginger's arm. I stared in horror for the space of a few moments. The bracelet was woven and had a circular, metal adornment in the center. It was an exact replica of the one that we'd found in Jason's apartment. Throughout the hustle and bustle of analyzing what Golden's citizens had to say about Dale's murder, I'd completely forgotten to show them the bracelet.

I cleared my throat. "Wendy, I think you'd better take a look at this."

Wendy leaned more heavily against the counter, waving her hand dismissively. "The guy wears solid black gauge earrings, so I already know that I don't like his taste in jewelry."

"Wendy," I repeated, taking on a sterner tone. "You need to look at this."

Wendy exhaled, turning her gaze reluctantly to the bracelet. Her expression changed the moment she laid eyes on it. "Oh my goodness! Is that . . .?"

"Go get the bracelet. It's in my purse," I ordered tightly.

Ginger's face was a mask of confusion. "What bracelet? What are you two talking about?"

"You'll see."

Wendy returned in record time holding the one piece of physical evidence we had in the murder case in the palm of her hand. I took it, holding it out for Ginger's inspection.

Ginger's bewilderment only deepened. "I don't understand. How did you get one of Graphite's bracelets? He doesn't give them away lightly. They're like his signature."

"His signature," Wendy repeated. "He dropped this in Jason's apartment while planting Dale's dead body at the foot of the bed. I guess that places Pea Gravel's autograph all over the murder case, huh?"

Ginger's mouth opened and closed like a codfish. "What are you saying?"

I gripped Ginger's shoulders with both of my hands. "Ginger, I'm really sorry to tell you this, but it means that Graphite was in Jason's apartment on the night of Dale's murder."

Ginger pressed a hand to her forehead, her breathing shallow. "That's not possible. It couldn't be."

Wendy and I shared a meaningful glance.

"I know it's hard to believe," I said. "But it's not just me making this up. I talked to one of the waitresses at the diner. Ben told me you three had been going there a lot."

Ginger nodded slowly.

"Margie said that when you went to use the ladies' room, she heard Ben and Graphite talking about some sort of secret scheme. Graphite was doing his best to convince Ben that carrying it out would help them to get revenge against Dale."

"I can't believe it," Ginger said, her eyes darting back and forth between Wendy and me. "He's brand-new in town. How would he ever think of doing anything like that?"

I turned wry eyes on Wendy. "Remember what you said about Graphite not being smart enough to orchestrate a murder on his own?

Turns out he isn't. Ben helped him. Besides, looking back, he really was over-the-top smug whenever anyone brought up Dale. He was acting from the beginning, being especially nonchalant in an attempt to throw us off his trail. It worked for a while, I'll admit. But the truth always comes out in the end." I looked back at Ginger with a sigh. "I'm sorry, Ginger, I really am. But we can't ignore this evidence. It looks like Graphite committed a serious crime. And I think Ben helped him." I shook my head. "I have to admit, the fact that he was constantly pursuing me was annoying, but I never would wish a prison sentence on him."

"Looks like he really wanted to date you, huh?" Ginger wrapped her arms around herself, her face falling. "And Graphite made me believe that he was such a great guy. Why do men have to be so . . . stupid?"

Wendy and I looked helplessly at each other as Ginger began to cry.

After a few moments, Wendy wrapped an arm around Ginger's shoulders in a rare show of empathy for our distraught friend. "Now, now, there's no need to go to mush over this. You didn't know that Graphite was capable of something like this. To be truthful, you really didn't know him at all."

I sent Wendy a look that warned her not to rub salt in Ginger's wound.

Wendy exhaled. "Everyone makes mistakes. But now you can do the right thing and help us get justice. You've been AWOL through most of our sleuthing, but that doesn't mean it's too late to jump on the bandwagon. Are you with us?"

To my surprise, Wendy's words seemed to do the trick.

Ginger sniffed, nodding in spite of the tears streaming down her face. "Yes, I'll help you. What do I need to do?"

I gripped Ginger's hand. "Come with us down to the station. They'll need to see the bracelet that Graphite gave to you." I looked to Wendy, who gave me an encouraging nod. "Then we can put this whole thing behind us. Justice for all. Right?"

Ginger studied Wendy and me tearfully for another moment before nodding again. "Yes. Justice for all." She lifted her chin, swiping at her cheeks as she squared her shoulders. "I'm ready to go to the station. It's time to tell Brenda that we closed the case."

Ginger strode to the front door, the bell jangling as she marched outside.

Wendy and I stared after her for a moment before looking at each other.

"We? All she did was flirt with the murderer the whole time we were investigating! Now she wants to act like she solved the case?"

I chuckled, looping my arm through Wendy's. "Yeah, but who cares? The important thing is that the case is closed." I put out my hand for a fist bump. "Girl detectives unite?"

Wendy's expression remained stubborn for a moment before she gave in, returning the gesture. "Girl detectives unite."

CHAPTER EIGHTEEN

*W*endy, Ginger, and I marched straight to the police station, the two condemning bracelets in our possession.

"You're doing the right thing, Ginger," I said as we made our way down the main street of Golden.

Ginger continued to hold her head high. "Yes, I know. No one gets away with criminal acts here in Golden. No one."

I looked over at Wendy, who was barely holding in her laughter at Ginger's soldier-like approach. It was rather dramatic, but I wasn't going to complain. I would certainly take it over tears and wailing. I'd known from the start that Graphite was no good and that Ginger was better off without him. I was pleased to see my friend accepting this reality with such fortitude.

It was no surprise that Mrs. Jeffries appeared seemingly out of nowhere, trotting up to join us on the sidewalk. That woman had a sixth sense; she always knew when something big was happening in town, no matter how hard you tried to fly under the radar. Yet, at the moment, I didn't mind her presence. This was a big moment for Wendy, Ginger, and me.

And for Jason.

He was about to be released from jail. My parents would have no reason to think badly of him. We'd solved the mystery, and I didn't care if everyone knew. In fact, I wanted them to. We'd done it!

"Where are you girls headed?" Mrs. Jeffries's eyes were bugged out with enthusiasm. Sure enough, her trusty binoculars were clutched to her chest.

Hate to break it to you, Mrs. Jeffries, but you won't be needing those anymore. The case is about to be closed.

"To put two murderers away, that's where we're headed," Wendy spoke up.

A few moments earlier, I would have sworn that Mrs. Jeffries's eyes couldn't get any bigger, but they expanded to the size of saucers. "You found out who killed Dale? And there are two? Who are they?"

Wendy tossed the eager bystander a smug grin. "You'll find out the answer when the police announce it. Soon, all of Golden will know."

Mrs. Jeffries continued to gawk as we made our way up the front steps of the police station. I caught sight of Mrs. Jeffries straining to see inside the police station with her binoculars just before the door shut. A police officer immediately stepped up to bar the door. Had he not, Mrs. Jeffries surely would have entered as well. We had evidence of paramount importance to present, and I was relieved to know that we were not to be disturbed.

We made our way straight to Brenda's desk.

Brenda's face was a mask of shock when Wendy, Ginger, and I arrived in front of her workstation. She stopped with her coffee cup halfway to her lips as she surveyed us. "What are you all doing here?"

Wendy straightened the collar of her pinstripe dress coat, flashing her sister a smile. "We've got big news for you, sis. It's about the Dale Meyers case."

"You found more evidence?" Brenda gasped as she set her coffee cup down on her desk with a clatter. Droplets of coffee splattered on her uniform, but she paid no heed, her eyes fixed on us.

"We sure did," Wendy responded, lifting her chin. She looked proud as a peacock.

Ginger, on the other hand, had lost the bravado she'd demonstrated back at *The Nugget*. It seemed her momentary pride over assisting in the execution of justice had waned. Perhaps she was thinking about Graphite's career. Sad as it was to cut his musical pursuits short with a prison sentence, I couldn't muster up much sympathy. Golden's newest member had ruined his own chances by going after Dale, and now he would have to live with the consequences.

Live . . . it's more than we can say for Dale Meyers. Unfortunately, Pea Gravel is about to bite the dust.

I hooked my arm through Ginger's in an attempt to reassure her. "We have two pieces of evidence that really turn things around in the investigation," I said. I reached into my pocket, producing the bracelet we'd found in Jason's apartment on the night of the murder.

Brenda leaned over her desk, her brow furrowed. "A bracelet?"

"One we found in Jason's apartment," I clarified. "We showed it to him after his arrest, and he has never seen it before."

Brenda leveled Wendy with a glare. "Oh, Wendy, you didn't . . . Did you two really sneak onto a *crime scene* after I told you that no one was allowed inside?"

Wendy crossed her arms stubbornly over her chest. "We sure did. But I'll have you know that if we hadn't, Jason might have been wrongfully convicted!"

Brenda raised her hands in surrender. "Okay, okay, I can see what you've come up with. You said there were two pieces of evidence. Where is the second?"

Wendy motioned proudly to Ginger, who held the bracelet Graphite had gifted her in the palm of her hand. "We're pleased to present to you the final bit of evidence that proves Graphite and Ben are guilty in the murder of Dale Meyers."

Brenda walked from behind her desk, taking both bracelets. "Still, the police have no way of knowing that these items truly belong to Graphite," she explained.

"Look at Graphite's wrist."

All eyes turned to Ginger, who hadn't said a word since our arrival at the police station. She squeezed my arm, and I found pride swelling inside of my chest that she'd mustered the bravery to stand against her new boyfriend. "You'll see Graphite always wears one just like this around his wrist."

"Golden is a small community," I said. "If someone in town owned bracelets like this, surely we all would have noticed them before. They're unusual. And Ginger is our jewelry expert! She knows the sorts of adornments available around here better than anyone."

Brenda continued to study the bracelets. "They are unusual . . ." She looked Ginger straight in the eyes. "What you mean to tell me is that if I go up to Graphite right now, he'll be wearing this exact bracelet?"

Ginger glanced at me before exhaling. "Yes, he will. I guarantee it."

"We couldn't have done it without Ginger," I piped up. I could see Wendy staring incredulously at me out of the corner of my eye, but I ignored her. "Without the bracelet she showed us, we wouldn't have the final clue connecting us to the murderers."

All eyes were drawn to the window when a loud commotion followed by a squeak interrupted the proceedings. We all looked just in time to Mrs. Jeffries, who had clearly found something tall enough to stand on in order to peer in through the window, topple off of her makeshift step stool and disappear beneath the sill.

Wendy rolled her eyes. "Mrs. Jeffries was desperate to get ahead on this case. Turns out peeking into windows isn't always the ticket, huh?"

Brenda's expression continued to hold a measure of doubt as she turned away from Mrs. Jeffries's disrupting presence, studying us with silent regard.

"And remember what I told you last night," I said. There was no chance I was going to let our investigating be in vain. I was going to make certain that Brenda saw the value of the evidence we'd provided. "Margie did hear Ben and Graphite discussing their plot. You can ask her yourself!"

Jason, get ready to be sprung from jail!

Brenda deliberated for a moment longer before nodding. "Yes, I believe that your evidence is strong enough to pursue. Looks like we need to speak with Ben and his new group member."

Wendy's pointer finger shot toward the door. "To the Wine Jug we go!"

My heart pounded with anticipation as I looked toward the

hallway leading to Jason's cell. I reached out to grab Wendy's coat sleeve. "Wait just a minute. There's one thing I need to do before we leave." I raced down the hall before Wendy had a chance to stop me. All I could think about was the beautiful ring Jason had offered me. When he was carted off to jail, it had made me believe that my chances of being happy were being locked away in the cell with him. But now I knew that wasn't true. We were going to be together. I could feel it!

Jason came to the front of his cell the moment he saw me. "Frannie! What are you doing here?"

I reached through the bars to grip Jason's hands. "What do you think I'm doing here? I'm here to get you out!"

Hope filled Jason's face. "Now?"

I placed my hand on his cheek. "Not this instant, but soon. All we have to do is go to the Wine Jug and prove that Graphite and Ben are guilty and you'll be free to go!"

Jason's frowned. "Graphite and Ben? Are you sure?"

"Sure as I could ever be," I answered. "Just watch, Jason. Soon you'll be out of this cell and back nerding out on your computer where you belong!"

Jason's expression intensified as he looked into my face. "And you? You told me to ask you again when all this was over..."

I gripped Jason's hands. "I know, and I'm sorry. But it was all too much. The thought of someone setting you up for murder!" I shook my head, searching for the right words. "I couldn't wait to be able to tell you I figured everything out. I wanted concrete evidence to prove your innocence. And now, I have!"

Jason nodded slowly. "Yes, Frannie, I can understand that. But there's one thing that we have to get straight now: marriage is a partnership. If we're going to be married, we have to work through every aspect of every problem we face *together*. That is . . . if you'll still take me after all that's happened." A sheepish look covered his face. "Will you still marry me even though I've done jail time?"

My heart swelled with love for Jason. I had to admit that there had been moments when I'd let my insecurities get the best of me. I'd made the mistake of wedding the wrong man once, and there was no way I wanted to do that again. But now I was certain. The problems that arose from the murder of Dale Meyers might have appeared to complicate things.

But for me, they didn't.

In fact, they clarified how I felt about Jason. I knew that he was the one for me.

I kissed him through the jail cell bars. "Of course I'll marry you. After all, if we can make it through an almost-murder conviction, we can make it through anything, right?"

The smile Jason gave me threatened to stretch off of his face.

I gave him one more kiss before heading back toward the front of the police station. "Be back soon with the keys to open up that jail cell. Don't go anywhere!"

He chuckled. "Don't worry, I'll be here!"

I laughed to myself racing back to join the others. I was ready for this. Ben might have thought that framing Jason would give him a chance with me, but he'd been wrong . . . *dead* wrong.

Now, I was coming for both him and Graphite and bringing the police with me.

Wendy raised her hands in the air when she saw me. "There you are! I can't believe you made us wait!"

"Jason and I had a little catching up to do," I replied.

Wendy shrugged in acquiescence. "I guess you're right. Did you get everything sorted out with your beau?"

I grinned. "Yes. Looks like we're going to have our happily ever after, after all."

Wendy waved away my answer. "Ugh, spare me the mushy details. I already had my fill of that lovey-dovey stuff tagging along with Graphite and Ginger."

I laughed. "You know, for a married woman, you're awfully anti-romanticism. But I'm willing to bet that you'll change your tune when I ask you to be my maid of honor."

Ginger jumped in front of me, her eyes wide. "Hey, what about me?"

I chuckled, grabbing one of her hands and one of Wendy's. "How do you two feel about being my co-maids of honor?"

Wendy and Ginger shared an uncertain look. It was true that they didn't always get along. But this case was proof that no matter what our differences were, we were all there for each other when it counted.

Wendy waited for a moment longer before offering a small smile. "Sure, I can go for co-maid of honor. What do you say, Ginger?"

Though Ginger was clearly emotional over everything that had transpired, she managed a smile of her own. She held out her hand to Wendy. "Co-maids of honor it is."

My friends shook hands, laughing.

Brenda glanced at her watch. "Alright, everyone, are we doing this or not?"

"We're doing it!" I exclaimed. "Let's go!"

Brenda led our charge out of the police station. Mrs. Jeffries struggled her way out of the bushes that had clearly broken her fall from the windowsill. I barely kept from laughing as she scampered to her feet and raced after us.

"Where are you all going now? Are you going to get Graphite?" Before any of us could answer, Mrs. Jeffries pointed to Ginger. "Are you all right sweetheart?"

I swung my arm protectively around Ginger's shoulders. "Ginger's just fine"

Mrs. Jeffries frowned. "It's that no good Graphite. I knew it! Did he work alone?"

Wendy, who'd clearly had enough of Mrs. Jeffries's meddling and sported zero tolerance for disruptions to our glorious moment, waved her hand dismissively in the overzealous woman's direction. "You'll have to wait and see, Mrs. Jeffries. We have the evidence to back it up and everything."

Mrs. Jeffries followed us all the way to the Wine Jug. However, Brenda turned to her before entering the establishment. "Mrs. Jeffries, I'm going to have to ask that you remain outside for the time being while we complete this order of business. I'm sure you understand."

Mrs. Jeffries crossed her arms, disgruntled as the rest of us filed into the bar.

Traditionally, the Wine Jug was dimly lit in order to lend a proper atmosphere. However, since it was currently being used only for band practice, the fluorescent lights illuminated the entire interior, eliminating every mysterious shadow.

Just like your sneaky misdeeds are going to come to light. Nowhere to hide now, boys.

Ben turned from the stage where Graphite and the other band members were setting up their instruments for practice. The emotion that dominated the band leader's face was surprise. However, I noted the look of fear that lingered behind his eyes. He knew why we were here.

Game over.

Ben's face registered shock as he watched Wendy, Ginger, and me approach alongside Brenda.

"Is there something I can help you with today, Officer?" Ben asked.

"Yes, there is," Brenda answered. "You can offer us your cooperation. While you're at it, you can ask your newest hire to cooperate too. Doing so will be in both your interests, trust me."

Ben's gaze flickered to me as Graphite made his way down from the stage. His black gauges looked more like bullet holes than ever now that we knew he was, in fact, the murderer.

Graphite swaggered over, offering Brenda a lopsided smile. "Hey Officer."

Brenda regarded Graphite with caution. "You're just the man we wanted to see."

Graphite grinned as if she'd paid him a compliment. "Oh yeah?" He held out his hand to Ginger. She turned her nose up at the gesture, holding her ground. A flash of confusion caused Graphite's nonchalant composure to crack for an instant. However, he quickly pulled himself together, blowing Ginger a kiss before turning his attention back to Brenda.

"The girls have something to show you," Brenda said.

Graphite's lips ticked up in the corners "Is that so?"

All eyes turned to Ginger as she stepped forward, holding out the bracelet he'd gifted her.

Graphite had the audacity to look hurt. "Ah, when I gave it to you, you told me you'd never take it off. Why aren't you wearing it, baby?"

"It sort of lost its charm when she found out that we'd discovered its doppelganger in Jason's apartment on the night of the murder," I said, stepping forward to present the condemning match.

Graphite's face grew pale as he stared at the bracelet in my hand.

"Recognize it, do you?" Brenda prompted. "The design is unusual. Never saw anything like it around town. That is, until you arrived."

The police officer's words were followed by pin drop silence. Graphite did his best to cover the bracelet on his wrist, but it was no use.

I looked from Graphite to Ben. Ben too had grown pale, guilt written all over his face. I couldn't help feeling sorry for him. His passion for me (which I still didn't quite understand) had led him down an extreme road. I knew that he was responsible for his own actions, but I blamed Graphite. That wannabe rock star was a downright bad influence on everyone he interacted with.

You sure had grandiose goals of becoming the next big star, didn't you? Turns out you're not a rock star, but a falling star.

"How could you, Graphite?" Ginger whispered, her eyes filling with tears.

Graphite tried to reach out to her again, but Ginger vetoed the attempted affection by taking a stubborn step backward, gripping my arm. "How could you trick me into thinking that you were a good man when you were really a *murderer*? And you framed the fiancé of my *best friend*! How *could* you?"

Graphite glanced around at all of us, his expression confused. However, by the time his gaze settled back on Ginger, he'd regained his composure. He squared his shoulders, tossing her that obnoxiously lopsided grin once more. "That Dale Meyers had it coming. The old geezer thought that he could push everyone in this town around. But not me. I figured a newcomer would be the best person to teach him a lesson."

Ginger shook her head, swiping tears from her cheeks. "You tricked me . . ."

"I didn't trick you, baby." Graphite's gaze swung to the rest of us. "In fact, if you all would open your eyes, you'd realize that I did you all a favor. Dale was disrupting everyone's plans for the Living History

Day celebration." A crack of laughter issued from the falling star's throat. "You all should be thanking me instead of interrogating me."

"Don't even try that," I said as fury at the fact that Graphite had nearly ruined Jason's and my chances for happiness bubbled to the surface. "You did this all for your own benefit. Don't pretend like you killed Dale because you wanted Mrs. Jeffries and Edmond to sing or Ms. DeLeon to be on the decorating committee for another year or Pierre's pastries to be the center of attention. Or even for Ben to have a chance with me."

"Golly gee, I just knew it!"

All eyes swung to the front window of the Wing Jug. Mrs. Jeffries might have been excluded from joining the interrogation, but she hadn't abandoned her post. Her face was pressed against the window-pane in true, snooper style as she gawked open-mouthed, clearly taking in every word.

Because the tension in the room was so thick I could have cut it with a knife, I held back the laugh that threatened to escape my mouth.

The pin drop silence ensued once more as everyone's attention shifted to the band leader who'd been standing in silence, looking more and more uncomfortable with each passing minute.

Ben refused to meet my gaze as he spoke. "I-I told Graphite that it wasn't a good idea. I didn't want to cause trouble. But he already wanted Dale out of the way because he was ruining our chances of making a big splash on Living History Day. I figured while he was at it . . ."

"Might as well frame my fiancé." I laughed dryly. "That's real smart, Ben."

Ginger sniffled beside me, choking back sobs.

"I couldn't think of any other way!" Ben's voice rose in desperation as he glanced appealingly in my direction. "I'd heard that things were serious between you and Jason. I was afraid that if I didn't act fast, I'd never have another chance. And then Graphite told me he planned to do away with Dale. He was the one who suggested that we join forces."

Ginger lost it then. Unable to hold back any longer, she released a wail, covering her face with her hands, her shoulders shaking as she dissolved into sobs. I slipped my arm around her.

Just hang in there for a minute longer, Ginger. We've just about got this one in the bag.

"Graphite, you really should have thought twice before you did your best to drag everyone down with you," Wendy barked.

"And the dumpster," I interjected. "Did you know that Pierre had been disposing his failed creations in the trash near Jason's place? That made it pretty easy to frame the baker if setting up Jason somehow failed. You were only looking out for yourself, Graphite."

"So much for fame," Brenda remarked. "Looks like you're not going to have quite as dazzling of a career as you thought. You have some jail time to serve first." She turned to Ben. "You too, Ben. I'm sorry that you got mixed up with this clown, but there's no getting around the fact that you're an accessory to murder. I'm going to have to place you both under arrest."

Graphite held up his hands. "Hey, now, let's not be hasty."

Brenda laughed, though her face was devoid of amusement. "Not a chance, buddy. You've been caught. Making a fuss will only complicate matters."

Without another word, Brenda radioed for Barney, who remained posted outside. In a moment, Barney had entered through the front doors. I saw Mrs. Jeffries craning her neck to see inside the Wine Jug before the doors shut once more. The news of the double arrest would be around town before we could even make it back to the police station.

But I didn't care. Wendy and I had done it. Jason was going to go free, and that was all that mattered.

Brenda came forward to cuff Graphite, sending her partner a nod. "Alright, let's take these two into custody. Looks like we have the wrong guy behind bars."

"Wait just a second!" Ginger cried, causing Brenda to pause. My friend sniffed loudly, drawing in a shaky breath as she stepped toward Graphite. She looked him straight in the eyes, her chin rising. "I despise what you did, Graphite. I'll never forget it. But I want you to know that I think you have talent. It's a shame you threw it all away."

"I was doing it for us, Ging," Graphite insisted even as Brenda slapped on the handcuffs. "I was doing it to pave the way for our future, baby."

"Alright, champ," Brenda said, patting him on the back as she nodded toward the door. "You've had your say. Now it's time to start down the path that's actually paved for you; off to the police station we go."

Barney and Brenda marched Ben and Graphite out of the Wine Jug, followed by Ginger, Wendy, and me.

Mrs. Jeffries trotted alongside us, grabbing my arm. "So it was Graphite!" she exclaimed. "I just knew I was right."

"Yes," I answered as we continued down the street. Shopkeepers were coming out of their shops to watch us. Arrests were rarely made in Golden, so this was bound to be the biggest happening of the year.

Apart from Dale's actual murder, of course.

"But you were under the impression that Ginger was involved," I said.

Mrs. Jeffries's eyes grew wide in her attempt at innocence. "I was only trying to be objective, Frannie, dear. You didn't really think I'd accuse Ginger of anything, did you?"

I shrugged as we arrived at the front of the station. Brenda held fast to a deflated-looking Graphite as she pushed open the door and escorted him inside. "I couldn't say, Mrs. Jeffries. But I can assure you that Ginger is in the clear. And so is Jason. It's time to get my fiancé out of jail."

CHAPTER NINETEEN

I entered the police station with my head held high, my heart pounding with anticipation. The other times I'd been here recently, I'd had to leave Jason behind when I left. This time, we'd walk out together. I would be content never to return. I had a feeling Jason would broach no argument. He'd undoubtedly had more than enough of this place.

"I can't believe you pulled me into this," Ben muttered to Graphite as they were escorted to their cells.

"No one was twisting your arm," Graphite retorted. "This is a free country, you know. Besides, I was trying to help you out by getting you a date with Frannie the Sleuth over there."

Ben shook his head as they came to a stop in front of the first cell. "Spare me the excuses. They didn't work on the police, and they aren't going to work on me. I never should have invited you to join *Oro Ignited* in the first place."

"I knew from the start that with a name like Graphite, he was definitely trying too hard," I chimed in. "It was a sure sign that something was up."

"Frannie!"

I turned toward Jason's cell with a ready smile. "We did it, Jason!"

Jason's eyes glowed with excitement as I reached through the bars to grip his hands. "We did it! You're going free!"

Brenda tapped me on the shoulder, her smile tinged with amusement. "If you'd just take a step back, we can get Jason out of that cell and make the appropriate swap."

My heart was full as I watched Wendy's sister unlock Jason's cell, sending Ben inside as Jason walked out.

Brenda stopped Jason and handed him something I couldn't see.

"Thank you, Brenda," he said.

"No hard feelings, right?" Brenda asked. "You know I was only doing my job."

"Sure," Jason said, wrapping his arms around my waist.

I inhaled his scent and pressed my forehead to his, finally feeling as if all was right with the world.

"Man, it's good to be out," Jason said. "Now I can finally get back to real life. And *us*."

A hush fell over the room as Jason's expression grew serious. He pulled away from me and dropped to one knee, revealing the little black box in his hand.

"It's the ring!" I breathed, suddenly realizing what Brenda had just handed him.

He smiled and gazed up at me, his heart in his eyes. "Brenda kept it safe for me. Frannie, I love you. I can't imagine my life without you."

Wendy dropped her head against Ginger's shoulder. "Oh my gosh, this is so romantic."

In spite of the fact that her life had been reduced to shambles by the day's events, Ginger conjured up a smile. "So now it's not disgusting, it's romantic?" She rolled her eyes. "It only took time behind bars and a murder for this romance to meet your criteria. You're a hard one to please, you know that?"

"Hush, you're ruining their big moment," Brenda admonished, clearly entertained by the turn this arrest had taken.

I looked back to Jason. His smile broadened. "Frannie, will you marry me?"

I beamed, yanking Jason to his feet so I could throw my arms around his neck. "Of course I will!"

"Congratulations!" Wendy and Ginger cried in unison.

"What a start to your engagement, you two." Brenda chuckled.

I laughed. "You can say that again."

"Congrats!"

We turned to see Mrs. Jeffries at the window, waving frantically. A moment later the binoculars were pressed to her face once more as she attempted to catch a glimpse of the ring.

"Should we save her the trouble of attempting to see the ring *through* the box?" Jason chuckled.

I thrust my hand toward him. "By all means!"

The occupants of the room—including Graphite and Ben, who appeared genuinely dumbfounded—watched with rapt attention as Jason slipped the beautiful, custom-designed ring onto my finger.

"Well!" Wendy burst out, tossing an arm around my shoulders. "Looks like we not only have the Living History Day celebration to plan, but another equally joyous occasion as well!"

"Living History Day is on?" Ginger exclaimed.

Wendy clapped her hands together. "I don't see why not! It's time for us to show Golden that nothing can stop our traditions. We'll triumph no matter what. Isn't that right?"

"Right!" Mrs. Jeffries cried from outside. We all exchanged glances before dissolving into gales of laughter.

I held tight to Jason's hand as he exited the jail. "We should go to the diner to celebrate!" I suggested.

"I second that!" Wendy piped up. "All of this excitement has given me an appetite for some good, old-fashioned house fries."

"You know, I'd love nothing more," Jason said, his tone regretful. "But I really should get home and answer some emails. I'll be lucky if I don't get fired for being MIA from work for so long."

I smiled up at Jason. "I understand. But trust me, they won't fire you. Just remember that you're their prize employee. Why else would they have offered you the opportunity to move to New York?"

Jason regarded me in silence.

I frowned. "What's the matter?"

Jason shifted his weight, clearly considering his words carefully. "You know, I had a whole lot of time to think while I was in jail." He chuckled. "Too much, actually. But it did give me a chance to figure out some things. Frannie, would you mind if we didn't move to New York?"

I blinked. "What? But the big promotion . . . I thought that it was your big break."

Jason shrugged. "That's what I thought too. But I've realized something: your work here in Golden at *The Nugget* is just as important." He gave me a chuck under the chin with one finger, offering me a fond smile. "And look at the great act of community service you've provided by solving the murder. Golden needs you."

I pressed my hands to my cheeks. "Do you really mean it?"

Jason dropped a kiss onto my forehead. "I do."

Ginger and Wendy assaulted me with hugs before I had a chance to say another word.

Wendy would have likely started discussing wedding plans and even what neighborhoods we should house hunt in then and there had we not been interrupted.

"Frannie!"

I whirled around to find my dad stalking toward me, his face cross.

"Speaking of my prestigious job at *The Nugget* . . ." I murmured to Jason with a chuckle.

"Where on earth have you been? You're my daughter, that much is true. But I still need you to arrive on time for your scheduled shifts."

I returned my dad's annoyance with a triumphant smile. "I think you'll forgive me when you find out what we've been up to."

My dad looked from me to Jason in confusion. "Jason, you're out."

Jason wrapped his arm around me, his smile broad. "Yes, sir, thanks to your daughter. She's quite the little detective."

Dad blinked. "The case has been solved?"

"It sure has!" Wendy exclaimed, looping her arm through my dad's. "And there's one more thing," she added, sending me a wink.

I laughed, holding out my ring. "Jason's name has been cleared and our engagement is back on!"

Dad's eyes narrowed as he became fully distracted by my unusual ring. "My, my . . . with a ring like that, your marriage is sure to be blessed."

Our group erupted into laughter at how easy it had been to obtain Dad's approval.

Seems a good piece of jewelry really can solve all of your problems, just like Mrs. Jeffries said.

Wendy began dragging Dad toward *The Nugget*. "Let's go have some champagne. You can put off work for a few minutes longer, can't you, Jason?"

Jason looked at me before throwing his hands up. "I guess it wouldn't do any harm. They don't serve champagne in the slammer, that's for sure."

I wrapped my arms around my fiancé's waist, tilting my head back to look up at him. "Never again, Jason. Never again."

CHAPTER TWENTY

$\mathcal{W}$hen Wendy announced that she would be taking the task of resurrecting our hopes for another memorable Living History Day celebration, no one in Golden argued. At this point, everyone was too grateful that the tradition would be allowed to continue to quibble over technicalities. The only requirement unanimously put forth by the citizens of Golden was this: those who were involved with the celebration annually would be guaranteed their usual posts. Wendy agreed, announcing that she wouldn't have it any other way.

Due to the fact that the preparations had come to a standstill in light of Dale's murder, Wendy had to work fast. She'd always been a business-minded type, but even so, I had my doubts about whether or not she would be able to pull it off.

Only a week after Jason's release from jail, I stood in the town square of Golden in complete awe. Wendy had not only accelerated the preparations to ensure that Living History Day could take place on the same day it did every year, but everything was just as it should be. Ms. DeLeon's decorations graced the square in all their garish charm, the alluring scent of Baker Pierre's luscious cinnamon rolls wafted through the air, and the cheerful voice of Mrs. Jeffries and Edmond emanated from the stage that had been set up next to *The*

Nugget's sales tent. *Oro Ignited* wasn't featured, of course, seeing as their leader was behind bars for murder, but Wendy had hired a small family band to take care of the evening entertainment. I had a feeling they would be a far cry from Pea Gravel and his rock star vibes. Though I hadn't heard *Oro Ignited*'s replacement yet, I was certain no one would have any objections to the new band, no matter what they sounded like.

So long as there's not a murderer in the mix, all is well.

But my favorite part was the costumes. I'd chosen a rosy-red gingham dress and a floral-patterned bonnet. I didn't much enjoy baking or cooking, but I felt as if I could accomplish both cheerfully with the crisp white apron I'd chosen tied around my waist. I knew that my outfit was quite fresh and pressed compared to the outfits the women in the rugged 1800s would have worn, but I loved it.

Dad, on the other hand, had gone all out with his miner gear, telling me that there was no point in dressing up if it wasn't going to be authentic. He'd made sure that his overalls and helmet featured a good, authentic layer of coal dust.

"Lemonade?"

I turned to find Jason at my elbow offering me a paper cup of neon-pink refreshment. "Ah, Ms. DeLeon's lemonade," I said, taking the beverage. "You know, I've never been much of a fan, but today I will drink gladly. Cheers."

Jason chuckled as he tapped his own cup against mine. "It feels pointless to complain about anything after almost losing it all, isn't it?"

I took a long drink before answering. "You've got that right. I never thought it was possible for me to be so excited to listen to the Jeffries sing or to buy one of Pierre's pastries. Or see all of these decorations. Had you noticed them?"

"*Noticed* them?" Jason guffawed. "They've been hurting my eyes since we parked the car."

I laughed. It was true, the neon-pink streamers strung along the tops of the tents were a bit much, as were the dozens of lawn ornaments situated near the bandstand. I remembered what Wendy had said about the decorations generally looking good for Living History

Day. They'd definitely gone downhill since last year and looked more like Ms. DeLeon's garden than town celebration adornments, but once again, I could think of no reason to complain.

I stood back to enjoy Jason's costume as I sipped my lemonade. He sported a plaid shirt with his jeans and wore a brown vest over the top. I liked the wide-brimmed hat that shielded his eyes. No one ever would have guessed he was a city boy by looking at him.

Jason downed the rest of his lemonade, tossing the cup in a nearby trash can before slipping his hand into mine. "I'm happy that Living History Day was allowed to continue, but I'm even more grateful that this whole mess didn't make you change your mind about me."

I pressed my cheek to his. It wasn't scratchy anymore, but nice and smooth. Rumpled nerd on his computer or my clean-shaven escort to the Living History Day celebration, I would take him. I knew now that I would have Jason in any form. "Never. Besides, how could I refuse you after being given such a great engagement ring?"

Jason rolled his eyes, but the smile tugging at the corner of his mouth gave away his amusement. My ring had caused quite a stir in town, and Mrs. Jeffries had already asked Ginger if she could replicate it so that Edmond could buy it for her for their anniversary.

"Speaking of jewelry, what do you say we see how Ginger's doing with her sales? She was up all night adding to her collection for the event."

Jason and I had just turned in that direction when one of *Golden Grub's* catering trucks pulled up.

"Looks like Mom's here," I said, downing the last of my lemonade. It was overly sweet, of course, but hit the spot today. "We should go say hello."

As if on cue, my mom swung out of the front seat of the truck, waving frantically at Jason and me. "Frannie!"

I waved back, waiting as she hurried toward us. The jacket of her black catering uniform flapped in the wind as she raced over. She straightened her chef's hat when she stopped in front of us.

"So, I finally get to see Jason out and about with my own two eyes!" Mom exclaimed.

Jason chuckled good-naturedly. "Seems jail couldn't quite hold me.

Good to see you, Jessica."

Mom glanced over her shoulder at the catering truck. Members of her crew were hard at work setting up the *Golden Grub*'s tent. She turned back to us with a wide smile.

"I hope that you two will stop by my tent for lunch. It's on me."

I smiled. "Thanks, Mom."

She turned to Jason then. "You know, I have to admit, I wasn't completely sure about you at first. After all, you swept into town and now you're taking my baby all the way to New York City. And when news came out that you'd been arrested for the murder of Dale Meyers . . ." Mom lowered her voice, leaning in. "I have to admit that I was a little concerned. But Living History Day is still on and here we are. Everything turned out alright, didn't it? What a way to end your last Living History Day in Golden before you leave for the big city lights of New York City."

I looked to Jason, who sent me an encouraging nod.

"Actually, we're not going to New York." I grinned up at Jason. "We've decided to stay here in Golden. I think we've had enough excitement to last us for a while without moving away, don't you think?"

Mom reached out, pulling me into her arms. "Oh, Frannie, that's wonderful news!" After we broke apart, she opened her arms to Jason. "Welcome to the family, son!"

Jason grinned at me over my mom's shoulder. "Thanks, Mom."

She stepped back, her expression content as she surveyed Jason and me. "Yes, I think you two will do quite well here in Golden. So long as you stay out of trouble," Mom added, wagging her finger in our direction. Before we could respond, she glanced at her watch. "Yikes, look at the time! Folks will be ready for lunch soon, and we aren't even set up yet! Remember, lunch is on me today, so you two come on back over once we're all set up, you hear?"

With that, she was off. It was Mom's way—here one minute and off the next. But we had her blessing, and that was the important thing.

My stomach rumbled as the sugary aroma drifting from Pierre's cart teased my senses. "Why don't we swing by Pierre's while we wait for Mom to get set up?" I suggested. "I want to grab a cinnamon roll or two before they're all gone."

The moment Jason and I arrived at Baker Pierre's tent, I realized that there was little danger of the Frenchman running out of baked goods. The tables were overflowing with more pastries than I'd ever seen in my life. My mouth immediately began to water.

"This is quite a spread, Pierre," Jason remarked, scanning our innumerable options.

Pierre's grin spread from ear to ear. "Only the best for Living History Day!"

"It's nice to see the trusty best sellers back on the menu, Pierre," I said. "I'd love to get two cinnamon rolls."

"Right away!" Pierre cried, immediately transferring the delectable rolls into a white box that would ensure the delicious frosting over the top was not disturbed. I shook my head inwardly as I watched Pierre introduce Jason to every one of the selections on the table.

How could I have ever thought he was the murderer? He'd never do anything that would get him locked away from his bakery, which jail surely would have.

By the time Jason and I departed from Pierre's tent, there was a long line of customers behind us. When we reached *The Nugget's* tent, there too were people waiting in line to buy up Ginger's jewelry and Dad's gold nuggets.

Ginger's eyes were glowing when we reached the table. "It's about time you two came around!" She swiped her hand across her forehead, dropping down into the folding chair behind her. "It's been crazy. Your dad just went to get more gift bags from the shop. I might sell out by the time the festival is over! Oh, but wait!" She ducked behind the counter, producing a flat, square box. "There was one thing I made sure to set aside. It's for you, Frannie. Happy engagement!"

I pressed a hand to my chest as I took the gift. "Ginger! You shouldn't have."

"Yes, I should." Ginger's smile faded, her expression turning serious. "I wanted to thank you for looking out for me. You know, with Graphite."

I shook my head. "Oh, Ginger, you don't have to thank me for that. What are friends for?"

"Oh, you know, for saving each other from Pea Gravel and other murderers. The usual," another voice said.

All eyes turned to Wendy as she leaned against one of the four poles holding the tent up. In her fashionably tailored, paisley frock and sky-blue heels, she looked every bit the event planner. Her face was positively glowing with satisfaction, whether over the success of Living History Day or the fact that we'd solved the case, I couldn't quite tell. Probably both.

"You've got that right," I answered wryly. "Love you both, but let's just hope I don't have to do anything like solve a murder again for quite some time."

"Go ahead, Frannie, open your gift," Jason urged.

I began to remove the lid but stopped, sending Ginger a suspicious look. "It isn't a bracelet to match Graphite's signature piece, is it?" I looked at Wendy to see her eyebrow quirked in my direction.

"Too soon?" I whispered.

"Yeah, maybe," Wendy answered.

"Oh, for heaven's sake, that's not what it is," Ginger piped up, waving off our concerns. "Open it and see!"

I popped the lid off of the box, gasping when I saw what was inside. "Oh, Ginger, they're gorgeous!" I carefully lifted one of the delicate, dangle earrings from the felt cushion, holding it up for all to see. It was pure gold—naturally—and featured a small triangle with a diamond set in the center.

"I thought they might go with your wedding dress," Ginger explained shly.

I reached over the table to grip my friend's hand. "They're perfect."

Wendy raised her cup of insanely pink lemonade in a toast. "To the happy couple."

"To the happy couple!" Ginger and a voice behind me echoed. I whirled around to find Mrs. Jeffries at my elbow.

"Oh, Ginger, I plan to come over to your tent and buy later this afternoon," Mrs. Jeffries exclaimed. "But first Edmond and I have another song to perform. You'll all come and listen, I hope?"

"We'll be right along, Mrs. Jeffries," Wendy replied.

"No way I'm missing it either, Mrs. Jeffries," Jason called after her. "Over my dead body." He looked at me, his brow lowered. "Too soon?"

I laughed at the way he mimicked my voice. "Yes, definitely."

Jason shrugged. "I tried. Come on, let's go listen to the Jeffries sing. It can't be worse than the lemonade, can it?"

I sent my fiancé a chiding look but couldn't quite hide the smile that peeked through. I gave in, laughing out loud as he pulled me toward the stage.

The joke might have been too soon, but he was right about one thing: there was no way I was missing this.

<><><>

Thank you for reading DYING FOR GOLD! I hope you love Frannie and her family as much as I do. Join Frannie's mom Jessica on her adventures in **RUNAWAY MURDER!**

In the historic town of Golden, not everything that glitters is...

Train aficionado, Jessica Peterson, may have found her dream job as the first female executive Chef of the Western Rails train. Problem is her ex-lover, is the Chief Conductor and he wants to turn the Summer BBQ Excursion into a Gourmet Champagne Brunch. Things turn contentious when online ticket sales double, thanks to Walter, the computer guru, and the results are in - it seems tourists are hankering for fancier feast.

Just when Jessica thinks she has a handle on her temperamental ex-lover and conductor, along with the hustle and bustle of her new job...

A body is found in the motorcar.

It's the computer guru, Walter. While plenty of people have motive, some of the strangers on the train carry dark secrets. The burden of getting the train back to the station before another person falls victim is on Jessica's shoulders.

Can she get everyone back safely, while figuring out whodunit?

. . .

136

CHAPTER ONE OF BUNDLE OF TROUBLE

A MATERNAL INSTINCT MYSTERY

Labor

The phone rang, interrupting the last seconds of the 49ers game.

"Damn," Jim said. "Final play. Who'd be calling now?"

"Don't know," I said from my propped position on the couch.

I was on doctor's orders for bed rest. My pregnancy had progressed with practically no hang-ups, except for the carpal tunnel and swollen feet, until one week before my due date when my blood pressure skyrocketed. Now, I was only allowed to be upright for a few minutes every couple of hours to accommodate the unavoidable mad dash to the bathroom.

"Everyone I know is watching the game. It's gotta be for you," Jim said, stretching his long legs onto the ottoman.

I struggled to lean forward and grab the cordless phone.

"Probably your mom," he continued.

I nodded. Mom was checking in quite often now that the baby was two days overdue. An entire five minutes had passed since our last conversation.

"Hello?"

A husky male voice said, "This is Nick Dowling . . ."

Ugh, a telemarketer.

". . . from the San Francisco medical examiner's office."

I sat to attention. Jim glanced at me, frowning. He mouthed, "Who is it?" from across the room.

"Is this the Connolly residence?"

"Yes," I said.

"Are you a relative of George Connolly?"

"He's my brother-in-law."

"Can you tell me the last time you saw him?"

My breath caught. "The last time we saw George?"

Jim stood at the mention of his brother's name.

"Is he a transient, ma'am?" Dowling asked.

I felt the baby kick.

"Hold on a sec." I held out the phone to Jim. "It's the San Francisco medical examiner. He's asking about George."

Jim froze, let out a slight groan, then crossed to me and took the phone. "This is Jim Connolly."

The baby kicked again. I switched positions. Standing at this point in the pregnancy was uncomfortable, but so was sitting or lying down for that matter. I got up and hobbled over to Jim, put my hands on his back and leaned in as close as my belly would allow, trying to overhear.

Why was the medical examiner calling about George?

"I don't know where George is. I haven't seen him for a few months." Jim listened in silence. After a moment he said, "What was your name again? Uh-huh . . . What number are you at?" He scratched something on a scrap of paper then said, "I'll have to get back to you." He hung up and shoved the paper into his pocket.

"What did he say?" I asked.

Jim hugged me, his six-foot-two frame making me feel momentarily safe. "Nothing, honey."

"What do you mean, nothing?"

"Don't worry about it," he whispered into my hair.

I pulled away from Jim's embrace and looked into his face. "What's going on with George?"

Jim shrugged his shoulders, and then turned to stare blankly at the TV. "We lost the game."

"Jim, tell me what the medical examiner said."

He grimaced, pinching the bridge of his nose. "A body was found in the bay. It's badly decomposed and unidentifiable."

Panic rose in my chest. "What does that have to do with George?"

"They found his bags on the pier near where the body was recovered. They went through his stuff and got our number off an old cell phone bill. They want to know if George has any scars or anything on his body so they can . . ." His shoulders slumped. He shook his head and covered his face with his hands.

I waited for him to continue, the gravity of the situation sinking in. I felt a strong tightening in my abdomen. A Braxton Hicks?

Instead of speaking, Jim stood there, staring at our blank living room wall, which I'd been meaning to decorate since we'd moved in three years ago. He clenched his left hand, an expression somewhere between anger and astonishment on his face. He turned and made his way to the kitchen.

I followed. "Does he?"

Jim opened the refrigerator door and fished out a can of beer from the bottom shelf. "Does he what?" He tapped the side of the can, a gesture I had come to recognize as an itch to open it.

"Have any scars or . . ." I couldn't finish the sentence. A strange sensation struck me, as though the baby had flip-flopped. "Uh, Jim, I'm not sure about this, but I may have just had a contraction. A real one."

I cupped my hands around the bottom of my belly. We both stared at it, expecting it to tell us something. Suddenly I felt a little pop from inside. Liquid trickled down my leg.

"I think my water just broke."

Jim expertly navigated the San Francisco streets as we made our way to California Pacific Hospital. Even as the contractions grew stronger, I couldn't stop thinking about George.

Jim's parents had died when he was starting college. George, his only brother, had merely been fourteen, still in high school. Their Uncle Roger had taken George in. George had lived rent-free for many years, too many years, never caring to get a job or make a living.

Jim and I often wondered if so much coddling had incapacitated George to the point that he couldn't, or wouldn't, stand on his own two feet. He was thirty-three now and always had an excuse for not holding a job. Apparently, everyone was out to get him, take advantage of him, "screw" him somehow. At least that's the story we'd heard countless times.

The only thing George had going for him was his incredible charm. Although he was a total loser, you'd never know it to talk to him. He could converse with the best of them, disarming everyone with his piercing green eyes.

Uncle Roger had finally evicted George six months ago. There had been an unpleasant incident. Roger had been vague about it, only telling us that the sheriff had to physically remove George from his house. As far as we knew, George had been staying with friends since then.

I glanced at Jim. His face was unreadable, the excitement of the pending birth diluted by the phone call we had received.

I touched Jim's leg. "Just because his bags were found at the pier doesn't mean it's him."

Jim nodded.

"I mean, what did the guy say? The body was badly decomposed, right? How long would bags sit on a pier in San Francisco? Overnight?"

"Hard to say," he muttered.

I rubbed his leg trying to reassure him. "I can't believe any bag would last more than a couple days, max, before a transient, a kid, or someone else would swipe it."

Jim shrugged and looked grim.

A transient? Why had the medical examiner asked that? George had always lived on the fringe, but homeless?

140

Please God, don't let the baby be born on the same day we get bad news about George.

Bad news—what an understatement. How could this happen? I closed my eyes and said a quick prayer for George, Jim, and our baby.

I dug my to-do list out from the bottom of the hospital bag.

To Do (When Labor Starts):
1. Call Mom.
2. Remember to breathe.
3. Practice yoga.
4. Time contractions.
5. Think happy thoughts.
6. Relax.
7. Call Mom.

OH, SHOOT! I'D FORGOTTEN TO CALL MOM. I FOUND MY CELL PHONE and pressed speed dial. No answer.

Hmmm? Nine P.M., where could she be?

I left a message on her machine and hung up.

I looked over the rest of the list and snorted. What kind of idealist had written this? Think happy thoughts? Remember to breathe?

I took a deep breath. My abdomen tightened, as though a vise were squeezing my belly. Was this only the *beginning* of labor? My jaw clenched as I doubled over. Jim glanced sideways at me.

He reached out for my hand. "Hang in there, honey, we're almost at the hospital."

The vise loosened and I felt almost normal for a moment.

I squeezed Jim's hand. My husband, my best friend, and my rock. I had visualized this moment in my mind over and over. No matter what variation I gave it in my head, never in a million years could I have imagined the medical examiner calling us right before my going into labor and telling us what? That George was dead?

Before I could process the thought, another contraction overtook me, an undulating and rolling tightening, causing me to grip both my belly and Jim's hand.

When my best friend, Paula, had given birth, she was surrounded mostly by women. Me, her mother, her sister, and of course, her husband, David. All the women were supportive and whispered words of encouragement while David huddled in the corner of the room, watching TV. When Paula told him she needed him, he'd put the TV on *mute*.

When I'd recounted the story for Jim, he'd laughed and said, "Oh, honey, David can be kind of a dunce. He doesn't know what to do."

Another vise grip brought me back to the present. Could I do this without drugs? I held my breath. Urgh! *Remember to breathe.*

I crumpled the to-do list in my hand.

Bring on the drugs.

CHAPTER TWO OF BUNDLE OF TROUBLE

A MATERNAL INSTINCT MYSTERY

*A*fter checking into the hospital and spending several hours in "observation," we were finally moved to our own labor and delivery room.

"When can I get the epidural?" I asked the nurse escorting us.

"I'll call the anesthesiologist now," she said, leaving the room.

Jim plopped himself onto the recliner in the corner and picked up the remote control.

"Hey, I'm having contractions here . . . they're starting to get strong. Aren't you supposed to be breathing with me?"

"Right," he nodded, flipping through the channels. "He he he, ha ha ha," he said in an unconvincing rendition of Lamaze breathing.

"Jim!"

"Hmmm?"

"I need your help now."

His eyebrows furrowed. "No TV?"

"Get me the epi . . . oooh."

He pressed the *mute* button. I sighed and gave in to the contractions.

<><><>

Another hour passed before the anesthesiologist walked in. I was horrified to see that he looked all of about seventeen.

"Sorry to make you wait," he said. "There was an emergency C-section."

"I'm just glad you're here now," Jim said.

The anesthesiologist laughed. "How are we doing?"

"She's doing great, really great," Jim said.

I would have told him to shut up, but that would have taken more energy than I had. Was this teeny bopper qualified to put a fifteen-inch needle in my spine? What *exactly* could go wrong with the epidural? I was about to chicken out when the nurse rushed in.

"Oh, here you are," she said to the anesthesiologist. "Let's go, before she's too far along."

Before I could back out, my torso and legs were blissfully numb.

The nurse placed a metal contraption, resembling a suction cup, on my belly and studied a monitor. "Do you feel anything?"

"Nope."

"Good, because that was a big contraction."

I smiled. "I didn't feel a thing."

The anesthesiologist nodded as he left the room. The nurse advised us to get some rest. Jim returned to the recliner and put the volume back up on the TV. I glanced at the clock: 3 A.M. already. Where was my mother?

My thoughts drifted back to George. What had his bags been doing on the pier? An image of a swollen corpse with a John Doe tag on its foot crept into my mind. I shook my head trying to dissociate the image from George and willed myself to think sweet, pink, baby thoughts.

I scratched my thigh to double-check the effectiveness of the epidural.

During my pregnancy, I had heard dozens of horror stories about infants with umbilical cords wrapped around their tiny necks, only to have the doctor push the infant's head back into the birth canal and perform an emergency C-section. In most of the stories the poor mother had to go through the C-section without any anesthesia. At least I'd already had the epidural.

At 7 A.M., the door to the room opened and my mother appeared, dressed in jeans and sneakers, with binoculars around her neck.

"How you doing?" she asked cheerfully. Without waiting for a reply, she reached up and put two hands on Jim's shoulders pulling him down to her five-foot-two level to kiss his cheeks. After which she handed him her purse and said, "I'm here now, Jim. You can sleep."

Jim smiled, clutched the purse, and happily retreated to his cot. Mom had adopted Jim long ago, even before we were married; it was a relationship Jim treasured since he had lost his own parents so many years earlier.

Just seeing Mom relaxed me. She placed her freezing hands on my face and kissed my cheeks. "Are you running a fever?"

"No. Your hands are cold. Where have you been? You look like a tourist," I joked.

"What do you mean?"

I indicated the binoculars.

"Well, I want pictures of my first grandchild!"

From Jim's corner came a snorted laugh, the kind that comes out through your nose when you're trying to suppress it. I laughed freely.

"What?" Mother demanded.

"They're binoculars," Jim said.

Mother glanced down at her chest.

"Oh, dear! I meant to grab the camera."

Jim relaxed, lying back on the cot.

Mom stroked my hair, then leaned over and kissed my forehead.

"You're frowning," she said.

"I'm worried about the baby. I'm worried about George." I looked over at Jim. His eyes filled with tears.

"George?" Mom turned to look at Jim. Jim covered his face with his hands.

Mom clucked. "Let's start with the baby. Why are you worried?"

I shook my head and took a deep breath. "Don't know. Nervous, maybe."

Mom patted my hand. "Well, that's normal. Everything is going to be fine. When did your labor start?"

"Around nine last night. Didn't you get our messages? Jim must have called at least three times. Where were you?"

Mom settled herself in the chair next to my bed. "I was at Sylvia's. She had a dinner party. There was a lady there who wanted to take home some leftover crackers. Can you imagine? They had sat out all night on an hors d'oeuvres plate. And she wanted to take them home!"

Mom knew me too well. She was making small talk, trying to distract me from thinking thoughts full of doom and gloom. It was working. I was actually laughing.

I peered over at Jim. His eyes were closed, a grimace on his face. He wasn't listening to Mom. He was stressed out. Mom followed my gaze.

"Now, what's happened with George?"

Jim flinched. "Let's not go there, Mom. We got a phone call, right, Kate? Just a call—"

I clutched Mom's hand. "Not just a call! It was a call from the medical examiner. They found a body in the bay and George's bags on the pier."

Mom eyes turned into saucers and she gasped.

"We don't really know anything yet," Jim said. "Let's not get all melodramatic."

Mom and I exchanged looks. "Everything will be fine, you'll see." She gave my hand a squeeze, then released it and folded her hands into her lap.

An awkward silence descended over us. Just then the nurse slipped into the room. "Don't mind me," she said. "I want to see how far along we are."

Jim watched the nurse, his brow creased in concern. I tried to remain calm, my attention returning to the beeping monitor reporting the baby's heart rate.

"Oh, goodness, the baby's practically here," the nurse announced.

I sat up a little. Mom clapped her hands in childish delight and Jim crossed the room to stand next to me.

"I'll call your doctor," the nurse said, turning to leave.

Mom started to follow her. "I'll be right back. I just need to feed my parking meter."

The nurse spun around and stared at Mom. "Don't leave now. You may miss the birth."

"The baby's coming that fast?" Mom asked.

"I hope I can get the doctor here in time," the nurse said, rushing out.

"I hope I don't get a ticket," Mom said.

I laughed. "Why didn't you park in the hospital parking lot?"

Mom shrugged. "There was a spot in front." She hurried across the room to the window, straining to get a peek at her car.

Jim tried to hide the smile that played on his lips. He leaned in close to me and whispered, "Here I am worried about you, the baby, and my brother the screw-up, while I could be worrying about really important stuff like getting a parking ticket."

I giggled. "Or who took home stale crackers from a party."

Our eyes locked. Jim's face broke into a huge smile. "I love you, Kate."

Mom came away from the window. "No ticket yet, that I can *see*."

Dr. Greene, my ob-gyn, popped into the room, her brown hair held in place with two tortoiseshell clips. She walked straight to my side, looking confident in her blue scrubs. She smiled into my face. "How are you doing, Kate?"

"Okay, I guess. I don't feel a thing."

She smiled wider. "That's the beauty of modern medicine. Just push when I tell you."

After about twelve minutes of pushing, Dr. Greene said the words I'll never forget in all my life: "Kate, reach down and grab your baby."

What? She wanted me to pull the baby out?

Startled by her words, I instinctively reached down.

There she was. I grasped my baby girl and pulled her to my chest.

I clutched her to me with a desperation I had never felt before, trying to press her right into my heart. Everyone else in the room seemed to fade into the background. My little angel, my little love.

She was the most beautiful thing in the world. Her round, pretty face was punctuated with a button nose, and strawberry blond hair graced the top of her head. Dark blue eyes peered at me, examining me with the wisdom of an old soul.

I realized Jim was crying. He reached down and enveloped the baby and me in his arms and I forgave him for muting the TV.

Out of the corner of my eye, I saw Mom pull a hankie from her purse and wipe a tear. "Don't worry, darling, I've already memorized her face. No one's switching her on us."

TO KEEP READING...

MATERNAL INSTINCTS

*B*ook 1 from Maternal Instincts Available at no cost...

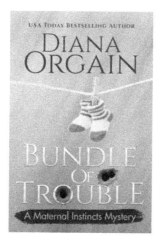

Click here to get your copy now.

GET SELECT DIANA ORGAIN TITLES FOR FREE

*B*uilding a relationship with my readers is one the things I enjoy best. I occasionally send out messages about new releases, special offers, discount codes and other bits of news relating to my various series.

And for a limited time, I'll send you copy of BUNDLE OF TROUBLE: Book 1 in the MATERNAL INSTINCTS MYSTERY SERIES.

Join now

ABOUT THE AUTHOR

$\mathcal{D}$iana Orgain is the bestselling author of the *Maternal Instincts Mystery Series,* the *Love or Money Mystery Series,* and the *Roundup Crew Mysteries.* She is the co-author of NY Times Best-selling *Scrapbooking Mystery Series* with Laura Childs. For a complete listing of books, as well as excerpts and contests, and to connect with Diana:

Visit Diana's website at www.dianaorgain.com.

Join Diana reader club and newsletter and get Free books here

CPSIA information can be obtained
at www.ICGtesting.com
Printed in the USA
LVHW012236290122
709583LV00004B/515